The Chalet School series by Elinor M. Brent-Dyer

Rivals of the
Chalet School

Elinor M. Brent-Dyer

Armada
An Imprint of HarperCollins*Publishers*

First published in 1929 by Chambers Ltd
First published in paperback in 1968 by
William Colllins Sons & Co. Ltd.
This impression 1992

Armada is an imprint of HarperCollins Children's Books,
a division of HarperCollins Publishers Ltd,
77–85 Fulham Palace Road, Hammersmith,
London W6 8JB

Printed and bound in Great Britain by
HarperCollins Book Manufacturing Ltd, Glasgow.

Contents

CHAPTER ONE

The New Building

Good Herr Braun came slowly down the lake-path, his hands clasped behind his back, his lips pursed round a cigarette. There was a peaceful look on his face, and his blue eyes were full of happiness as he gazed at the lake, bluer even than they. Suddenly, as he paused outside the high withes-and-stakes fence that surrounded a certain wide piece of land and two chalets, he heard a clear bird-like whistle. At once he removed his cigarette and swept off his hat; for Herr Braun, though he was only a fat old Austrian hotel-keeper, was a gentleman at heart, and he knew the whistler.

She appeared a moment later − a slender girl of fifteen, with a pointed face, shadowed by lank black hair cut in a deep fringe over her forehead. She was pale, but it was a healthy pallor, and her black eyes were bright with intelligence and twinkled merrily as she saw him. "*Grüss Gott*, Herr Braun," she cried. "Isn't it a glorious day today?"

"*Grüss Gott, Fräulein* Joey," he replied. "So you have returned to us once more?"

Joey Bettany nodded, and turned to fall into step beside him. "Yes; came home last night, and found the whole family waiting for me. I've just been up to the school to see Mademoiselle, and to hear the news. She tells me we have grown again, and will be just seventy girls this term even though there was such a clearing-out last. Heigh-ho!" she ended with a sigh.

"Change must come sometime, Fräulein Joey," said Herr Braun.

"Oh, I know that. The trouble is, changes aren't always as pleasant as one would like."

Herr Braun nodded his agreement with this sentiment, and they walked slowly on.

"What's that building over there?" asked Joey suddenly stopping in her walk to point towards a big new chalet that had risen at the Buchau side of the lake, just opposite the Chalet School.

Herr Braun shook his head. "Ah, *mein Fräulein*, that, I cannot tell you. It has been built during your vacation, and no one knows what it is. Not another hotel, I think, for it has partitions with glass in them — I have seen all over it; the builder is cousin to my wife."

"P'r'aps someone from Innsbruck, or Kufstein, or Vienna, making a summer home," said Joey, "though it looks rather large for that. Are you going on, Herr Braun? Then I must turn. I promised my sister that I wouldn't be late for *Mittagessen*." She smiled at him, showing white even teeth, and turned to go home to the chalet where her sister Madge, and the latter's twin brother with his wife, and the four babies that would learn to call her "Auntie Jo" sooner or later, were spending the summer season.

Jo had seen much of Dick and Mollie and their three children. They had come during termtime, and as soon as term was over she had gone off to Belsornia with her great chum the little Crown Princess, who had spent two happy terms at the Chalet School as a pupil, till the death of her grandfather had brought her, heir-presumptive, to the throne of Belsornia. Princess Elisaveta had begged to be allowed to stay on at the chalet till the year was up, at least, but the Government would not hear of it.

But, come what might, the little Princess had no idea of forgetting her school-friends, and Joey Bettany least of all, for Joey had saved her from the evil of falling into the hands of her father's cousin, a man with a twist in his brain, who had attempted to kidnap her and hold her a hostage till he had got what he wanted out of the old king. Thanks to Joey, Elisaveta had escaped, and the pair had got back to the Chalet School not much the worse for their adventure.

She ran lightly along the lake-path, past the Kron Prinz Karl

Hotel, which belonged to Herr Braun, and turned up the narrow path leading up the valley to the mountains. She passed over the little rustic bridge which was swept away nearly every spring when the thaw came, and over the little stream which, although today, it gurgled merrily over its stony bed, rose and swelled in flood seasons to a mountain torrent, carrying down with it all that came within its reach, and, furiously angry, tearing at the banks with its greyish waves. The path led through a flowery meadow, though, since it was now September, the flowers were fading, and so to the chalet which was their home for the present. A pleasant, wooden erection it was, with window-boxes full of geraniums and marguerites, and windows wide-open to the sun and the fresh wind.

"Here comes Joey!" cried a man's voice, and she ran to meet her brother-in-law, Doctor James Russell, who ran a sanatorium up on the Sonnalpe, and who had come down that morning specially to welcome his young sister-in-law home. "Well, you monkey! Had a good time? Goodness me, girl! — When do you intend to stop growing? You're taller than Madge as it is!"

"A good thing, too!" she retorted. "Do you realize that I'm to be a prefect this coming term?"

Her sister rose from her seat and came to them, her small son in her arms. She smiled up into the clever face with its sensitive mouth and beautiful eyes. Madge Russell was pretty with a delicate, elusive prettiness that came to mean more to most people than the Irish beauty of her sister-in-law, Mollie Bettany. Her deep eyes were filled with tenderness, now, for her baby-sister, whom she had mothered ever since the frail infant had been put into her arms nearly sixteen years before. "Just in time for dinner, Joey," she said. "How is everything at the chalet?"

"All right, I think," said Joey easily, as she took her tiny nephew from his mother's arms. "What a weight he is, Madge! How on earth do you manage to trot him round all day as you do?"

"Indeed I don't!" returned Madge indignantly. "I've more sense than *that*! He spends a good deal of the day in his pram, I can assure you! I don't believe in spoiling babies; and David knows that when he's put down, he has to stay there!"

Jo looked round the room disgustedly. "Nothing to eat *yet?*"

"Not for half an hour," replied her sister. "It's only half past twelve now. You don't want *Mittagessen* till one, surely, after the *Frühstück* you ate at nine?"

"But my watch says five-to," objected Joey, passing over the insult about breakfast.

"Then it must be fast. Give me David, and go and make yourself respectable. You look as if you had been dragged through a hedge backwards! By the time you are ready — you can change your frock while you are about it — *Mittagessen* will be on the table. Trot off!"

Jo grimaced at her, resigned the baby to his mother, and went off whistling piercingly, to reappear twenty minutes later, looking decidedly better for the change and general tidying she had undergone.

"Jem, what's that new chalet being erected for?" she demanded, during a pause in the meal. "I asked Herr Braun, but he doesn't know. Do you?"

The doctor shook his head. "No idea at all. I've wondered, though."

"Why shouldn't we go for a tramp round the lake presently, and see if we can find out — you and I?" suggested Dick. "And we can call at the Kron Prinz for Humphries and the Robin to come. I suppose you two" — he turned to his wife and sister — "will want to stay with the kids, but Joey might come."

"Good idea," said Jo.

"You might as well," said his wife. "I've been aching to know ever since they began. Of course Madge and I couldn't leave the babies, Dick. Don't be so absurd! We'll stay at home and look after them while you folk go off on an exploring expedition."

"Don't be too late, though." warned her sister-in-law. "And do remember that the Robin is only small, and tires rather quickly. Jem, do you think she had better go?"

Her husband shook his head. "No; since you ask me, I don't. But she can come up here till we come back. She'll be quite happy with the babies and you."

"Then buck up, and get this over, and I'll run round to the Kron Prinz Karl and tell them," said Joey, eating with reckless speed.

They laughed, but they fell in with her wishes, and twenty minutes later saw the elders drinking their coffee, while Joey raced down the path to the Kron Prinz Karl, where were staying Captain Humphries, secretary to her brother-in-law's sanatorium, and his small motherless daughter, Cecilia Marya, better known as the Robin. They had just finished *Mittagessen* when she burst into the room, which was nearly empty, for most of the visitors had already left and the season was at an end.

When she saw Joey, the Robin dropped her napkin and darted from her seat, to be caught up and kissed. "Joey — Joey!" she cried. "What do you do this afternoon?"

"Going for a walk with Dick and Jem," said Joey, setting her down, and coming to shake hands with Captain Humphries. "They want to know if you'll come, too, Uncle Ted? Madge and Mollie want the Robin to stay with them, as they are thinking of going rather a long way, and she might be tired. Will you?"

Captain Humphries laughed at this somewhat involved explanation, and nodded. "Oh yes! We'll come with pleasure — won't we, Robin? Just give us five minutes to get ready and then we'll be off with you."

He held out his hand to his little girl, and they left the room, Joey seating herself on an empty table to await their return. When they came back, they found her deep in conversation with Frau Braun, who adored her, and thought there was no one in the world like her.

"Ready, Joey?" called the Captain.

11

Jo slid down from her perch, submitted to being affectionately embraced by the warm-hearted Tyrolean, and went out with them, her arm through 'Uncle Ted's,' and the Robin clinging to her other hand. "We're going to walk round the lake," she said, as they made their way up the little path. "We're all dying to know what that new chalet is being built for, so we're going to take it in our stride, and then go on — to Tiernkirche, I think."

"But me, I could walk that far," protested the Robin.

Joey said lovingly, "Madge and Mollie want you to stay and help them with the babies."

"But I want to be with *you*," said the Robin. "Soon school comes, and then I am not ever with you, Joey, and it is not nice."

"I'll be back before your bedtime, and I'll promise to be with you all tomorrow," said Jo.

"I s'pose that must do," sighed the Robin.

"And you'll be able to help to bath the babies," put in her father persuasively.

That helped matters a good deal, for there was nothing which delighted the Robin more than to help with the bathing of the four babies, and it was a treat she didn't often get. So she cheered up, and it was a smiling small face beneath the thick black curls that was raised to 'Tante Marguérite's' when Mrs Russell drew her close for a kiss.

The Robin's mother had died three years before this story opens, and the little girl herself was also frail, so that they were obliged to forego many desired treats because they were afraid of taxing her strength.

Joey kissed her good-bye, and renewed her promise to spend the next day at the Tiernsee, and then the quartette went out to see what they could find out about the new building. Their way lay round the south end of the lake, across the water-meadows, whence the last crop of coarse hay had been carted the previous week, and then back on the lake-road to Buchau, a tiny hamlet on the opposite side of the lake from the Chalet School. That was situated at Briesau, a triangular spit of land that ran up into the mountains on the western borders, and, as they turned, they could see the two houses — the Chalet, and Le Petit Chalet — rising above the fence which hid them from the view of strangers. Three-quarters of an hour's brisk walking brought them to Buchau and the new chalet, which stood, bare and gaunt in its newness, not far from the *Gasthaus* or hotel, which, with the tiny chapel and one or two huts, made up the hamlet of Buchau.

Standing nearby was a tall woman, gaunt as the house itself, and clad in grey tweeds. She turned and looked at them as they drew near with a certain amount of interest in her keen eyes. Then her glance fell on Joey. She left her stand, and came over to them. "Forgive me stopping you," she began, in a somewhat hard metallic voice, "but I see that you have a school-girl with you, and I could not miss the opportunity of presenting you with one of my prospectuses, in case you should wish her to remain here for the sake of foreign languages."

"Prospectuses?" gasped Captain Humphries, to whom she had addressed herself, seeing that he was obviously the eldest of the party.

"Yes; I'm bringing my school here from England as an experiment," she said, "and I thought you might like your daughter to come here. We shall make a special feature of foreign languages," she went on, as the quartette remained silent, mainly because their breath had been taken away by the unexpectedness of it all, "and there is nothing that gives a girl such aplomb and savoir-faire as travel or sojourn abroad in a strange land."

At this point Joey recovered her breath and promptly spoke for herself. "Thank you, but I've lived here for three years now, and I speak German and French as well as I do English, and my Italian isn't so dusty, either."

13

The lady stared. 'But what about other lessons?'' she demanded sharply. "Languages, even when one speaks them fluently, are not everything.''

"*Don't* I know it!'' groaned Joey.

"And the best of governesses cannot be compared with the good that a school and all the competitions of school-fellows give a girl.''

At this point Jem interfered. "Thank you, Madam,'' he said. "My sister-in-law goes to the Chalet School, which you can see on the other side of the lake.''

"Oh yes,'' interrupted the lady; "I heard there was one here, but run by a Frenchwoman, and we all know what *their* ideas on education are! Now here, the girls will be under English supervision, and will learn good solid facts.''

Joey was furious, and was prepared to say what she thought, but Jem, guessing at this fact, went on quietly. "The school in question is run by a particularly efficient Head, and her staff are nearly all English. Incidentally, my wife, who began the school, still takes a great deal of interest in it; and I can assure you that even were it not so, we should never dream of removing our girls from a school we know and approve to one of which we know nothing at all.''

The lady opened her eyes, and then her lips thinned. "I see,'' she said. "In that case, there is no more to be said. I will wish you a very good afternoon.''

The three gentlemen raised their hats, and they all went on, Jem holding Jo's arm in a warning grasp, for that young lady was well-nigh dancing with rage, and he had no wish to create a feud between the two schools.

They were well on the way to Seehof, the next hamlet, before his grip relaxed, and Joey was able to voice her opinions of the new school, its Head, and all her works. "It's a downright mean thing to do!'' she proclaimed. "To try to sneak pupils away from other schools like that! And she's got a good nerve to come here and start a school when there's one already!"

"Steady on, old lady," said Jem. "We haven't bought up the lake-side, you know. If the good lady thinks she can run a second successful school here, she has every right to try. But for Heaven's sake, Joey. don't be rude to her, and do try to control your tongue a little when you meet her. It will only make things very uncomfortable all round if you misbehave. I should have thought you'd be rather pleased at the idea. It will mean that you can play them at matches, and that's what you folk have been wailing for for along enough."

"All the same, it's cheek!" insisted Jo.

Dick burst into a roar of laughter. "Keep you hair on, my child," he said, as soon as he was calm again. "Don't start any blood-feuds or guerilla warfare. I implore you, or we may have that old stick walking off with you to imprison you in her deepest dungeon — I'm sure she looks quite capable of it!"

Jo shrugged her shoulders. "I'm not going to make a goat of myself — you need't be afraid of *that!* For one thing, I'm a prefect this term. For another, she'd only say things about the school if I did, and I won't have that happening. All the same, I'd have liked her better if she hadn't tried to get me in such a sneaky way."

They agreed with her, though they had no intention of saying so, and Madge, when Jem told her all about it that night, agreed also.

CHAPTER TWO

The New Term Begins

"Joey — Joey Bettany! For goodness sake come here, and tell us the truth of this wild story Frieda insists on spreading! Is it really correct that another school is being started at the other side of the lake? If it's so, who's doing it? And what sort of school is it?"

Joey Bettany, with her arms full of clothes belonging to Simone Lecoutier, one of her closest friends, paused on her way to the Green dormitory in response to this agitated speech from Margia Stevens, one of the middles.

She put down her load and resigned herself to the inevitable. "Well, it's true enough that there's another school starting — over there at Buchau." She waved an explanatory hand towards one of the big windows that looked across the lake. "It's to be run by an Englishwoman named Browne. Jem and Dick and Uncle Ted and I went for a walk the day after I got back from Belsornia, and she met us, and actually had the cheek to suggest that I should leave *here* and go *there!*" Joey's voice thrilled with indignation at the memory. "She looks like — like — well, like a gorgon, and I'm sorry for any poor creature that gets into *her* clutches! She had a school in England somewhere, and had the bright idea of moving it out here. So she's built that new chalet over there, and they start this term."

"Goodness!" gasped Margia. "Another school out here. What a lark! But what a nerve to try to get you from us! What did you say?"

"Didn't get a chance of saying," returned Joey ruefully. "Jem was on to me like a shot, and did all the saying that was done. Oh, and he says we aren't to start any blood-feuds or things like that. Well, they're at one side of the lake, and we're

16

on the other, so I don't suppose we shall come across them very much — especially as this is the Christmas term, and there won't be much chance of getting around, once the winter comes. They say it's going to be an early winter, too. Lots of the cattle have come down from the alms already.''

''Already? I say!'' Margia's face fell. ''That's bad. isn't it? It means a thin time for the folk here if that's the case. And those salt-mines they were talking about at the end of last term can't have begun yet, so what's going to happen?''

Joey shook her head. ''Goodness knows! Madge was down at the Piensches yesterday, to say that they could send up Zita when they liked. Mercifully, her pups arrived in the season and they all sold well; so if we take care of the old dear, they won't do so badly. Madge thought some of us might get up a show of some kind, and ask all the visitors left to come, and have a collection. Then we can help any desperately needy cases.''

''But there's such a lot ot them,'' said Margia seriously. ''Even if we made a decent sum that way, it wouldn't go far.''

''We can have a box, and put some of our spending money in it each week,'' suggested Ilonka Barkocz, a pretty Hungarian child of fourteen. ''If we all promised to give half each week, it would help, would it not?''

''Oh. it'ud help, I suppose,'' said Jo, who was occupied in gathering up Simone's wardrobe as she spoke. ''Even so it's likely to be a hard winter.''

She finished her task, and departed to the upper regions of the house, where the seniors had their dormitories, and the middles looked at each other. Most of those present had been at the Chalet School for two winters, and they knew what a terrible thing an early winter was for the people round about the lake. Most of them depended on the summer season for their livelihood, while the rest were herdsmen, who watched the cattle up in the high alms or alpes during the summer months, but had to come down with them when the cold weather came. The cattle were housed in great byres and sheds, and only one man was required to care for them in place of two who had kept guard over them up in the mountains. The rest had to manage as best they could till the thaws had ended, and the warm sun called them again to the alms. Starvation was never very far from the door when winter came early, and with starvation might come pestilence. The girls had all been well-informed on this subject, for one of the aims for the Chalet School was to teach them to think of others. No wonder Joey's latest news had driven the new school out of their heads for the moment!

Meanwhile, that young lady had gone on, up the steep narrow stairs, to the big pleasant room with its green curtains, where the prefects slept. She was greeted by a derisive chorus, which wanted to know what had happened to her, since she had taken twenty minutes to get Simone's frocks and come upstairs.

"Did you sit down and have a nap on the way?" demanded the head-girl, a stocky young person, with a sensible, cheery face.

"Or did you let all fall to the bottom and so oblige yourself to go back to get them?" asked Marie von Eschenau, a strikingly lovely girl of fifteen.

Joey dumped them down on their owner's bed, and then turned and faced them. "Neither! Margia came shrieking to know what Frieda's story of the new school meant, so I stopped to tell them, and also to break the news that we are going to have an early winter. Then I left them, and came on up here. Anyone seen Miss Carthew's successor?" she added.

"I have," said Mary Burnett, the head-girl.

"Oh! What's she like?"

"Very much on the spot, I should think."

"How do you mean?" demanded Joey.

"You'll find out when you meet her," said Mary darkly.

Joey laughed and stretched out her arms. "Well, it looks like being an interesting term, at any rate, doesn't it? Heigh-ho —

I wish old Grizel were still here! It doesn't feel like school without her."

Mary nodded. "True enough. And *don't* I wish I could just be a meek and mild middle again, and not a prefect!"

"You were one last year." said Frieda Mensch, a quiet girl, with the fair plaits, blue eyes, and apple-blossom colouring of her North Tyrolean ancestry.

"Yes," put in Simone Lecoutier, nodding her smooth black head. "It is for you easy, Mary; but for us who are new to the work, it is not so pleasing."

"You'll manage all right," said Jo. "You never want to do wild things − or hardly ever. I can only once remember you doing anything out of the way." Her black eyes lingered thoughtfully on Simone's neatly shingled black hair.

The French girl wriggled impatiently. "I wish you would forget, Jo. It is not *gentil* to remind one so often of the follies one has committed."

The others laughed. Some of Jo's own doings had been as wild as they could well be. Simone's one lapse, to wit, the cropping of her hair in a sudden fit of jealousy some three years previously, was mild compared with more than one of her friend's escapades.

"It looks very nice," said Mary soothingly. "And while you are at school, I do think it is quite a sensible plan."

Marie shook her own lovely curls of warm gold back from her face. "I wish my parents would think so," she said. "But they will not hear of it. Wanda wanted to cut hers after she was married, but Friedel was horrified and made her promise that she never would."

"I should think *not*!" retorted Jo, aghast. "Wanda without her curls would be awful. You aren't bad, Marie, but we've never had a girl so beautiful as Wanda, and I don't suppose we ever shall! I wish she hadn't married," she went on. "It seems so awfully elderly for our girls to be married. Just look at Gisela! Three years ago, she was our head-girl, and a jolly good one too. Now, she's married, and has settled down to keeping house and darning Gottfried's socks. Then Wanda goes and marries Friedel, and has a flat to run. Bernhilda is engaged, and will be married in December, and even if Kurt *is* your brother, Marie, and quite decent — I must say I think they needn't all be in such a hurry to grow up." She finished with a little quiver of her sensitive lips which the others didn't see.

The truth was that Joey Bettany was beginning to realize that she, too, was beginning to grow up, and she hated the idea. At that period of her existence she would have greatly preferred to remain about fourteen. But she would be sixteen in November, and she knew that the time for monkey-tricks, such as had rejoiced her soul, must end now.

The others, not being given to introspection, laughed at her speech.

"Jo would like to stay a babe for ever!" said Mary. "It can't be done, Joey."

"But I think it will be very pleasant to grow up," said Marie. "Then I, too, shall be betrothed, and have a good fine husband as Wanda has. I shall like to make my own home pretty and pleasing to my husband, and I shall try to have everything as he likes it."

Shy Frieda, voiced no opinions, but she was a well-brought-up girl, who had been taught that, however much knowledge one may gain while at school, yet the chief knowledge for a girl is home-making.

Joey looked round at them with brilliant eyes. "What are you all going to do when you leave school?" she asked; "not just ragging, I mean, but seriously."

Mary took the lead. "I want to go to the Sorbonne, and take my 'bachot.' Then I shall try to get a post for modern languages in some good school, and when I've taught a few years, I should like to be head-mistress in a big high-school."

20

"But do you never wish to wed?" asked Marie, open-eyed.

Mary shook her head. She was that rare thing, a genuine student, and she knew that, for her, the ambition she had just spoken would bring the greatest happiness.

"Well, I must go home for a time," said Marie slowly. "But soon, I hope, I shall wed, and have a happy home. That is all I desire."

"Me, too," said Frieda, soft-voiced.

"Now, Simone?" said Joey.

Simone nodded her head, "I, too, hope to go to the Sorbonne, and gain my 'bachot.' Then I shall teach for some years. But I hope I shall not teach all my life, for that I should not like. I want a home to make happy, like Marie and Frieda; but not too soon. My parents are poor; and I would wish to work and make money for them, that when they are old they may live in comfort and ease. And you, Joey? What is it that you wish to do?"

"Write," said Joey briefly.

"But you will wed later?" said Simone.

Joey shook her head. "I can't imagine it," she said simply.

"And I pity any man that marries you with the idea of your making a happy home for him," said Mary ruthlessly. "You haven't the rudiments of tidiness in you to begin with; and your mending is a sight to behold!"

At this moment there was a tap at the door, and then the Robin entered to summon them to the big room in which all formal meetings took place, as Mademoiselle Lepâttre wanted to speak to the whole school together.

They got up from the beds on which they had been sitting, and trooped off downstairs, the conversation forgotten for the time being, and settled down in their places. The babies, as the Junior House were called, curled up on the floor in front; the middles sat on wooden chairs round the room, and the fourteen seniors seated themselves in wicker chairs, with the eight prefects on the right hand of the big chair which Mademoiselle would take when she came in. The staff sat on the left, and most of them were already there, including Miss Stewart, successor to the popular Miss Carthew who had left the previous term to be married, and a new importation, Mademoiselle Lachenais, who was to take the modern languages in the school. Hitherto, Mademoiselle Lepâttre had attended to this department herself. But the ever-increasing duties of headmistress had made her decide to give up the work, and get someone specially to do it. The visiting staff, Mr Denny, the singing-master, and Herr Anserl, who taught piano, were not there, of course, but the rest, with the exceptions of Miss Durrant, the junior-mistress, and Matron, were seated in state when little Mademoiselle Lepâttre opened the door, and came in quietly.

She took her seat, and signed to the girls to sit down again. Then she began her speech. ''We are all very pleased to see you here again, *mes filles*, and also to welcome all newcomers to our midst. There will be changes this term, as you know. With the departure of Grizel Cochrane we have lost the last of our ''big'' girls, who were also our first girls. But we still have Josephine Bettany, Simone Lecoutier, Frieda Mensch, and Sophie Hamel among our seniors, and there are others among our middles. To you I say, hold on to the ideals that those others have left with us that, when you in your turns must leave us, those ideals shall be so well established among us that they shall never falter, never grow less.

''This term, as some of you know, I am giving up the actual teaching in the school, for there is much else that needs my attention. But I shall still retain my lessons in literature of all countries, and so I shall see all of you at least twice a week in the intimacy of the classrooms. In my place, we have Mademoiselle Lachenais, to whom we accord a warm welcome.' Miss Stewart comes to take the place of Miss Carthew, and we shall have, next week, yet another mistress to greet in Miss

Nalder, who will take you all for gymnasium and games.''

There was an audible gasp at this, for no one had even known that such an idea was being entertained, and keen people looked at each other with grins of pure delight. If only there had been other schools which they could challenge at games, their cup of joy would have been full. Mademoiselle knew what they were thinking, and she smiled as she went on.

''One other piece of news I have for you. It is that a new school is beginning on the lake shores this term. At Buchau, a Miss Browne has built for herself a house to hold the school she had in England, and next week her girls and staff will be here. She has already been to converse with me, and has asked that you may play matches against her girls in hockey and netball, and, in the summer, in tennis and cricket. I have agreed for the present, and so, when the new school begins, you will be able to challenge them and have your matches. But, I have one thing to say to you all. I do not wish, nor does Madame, that there should be any quarrelling with these strangers as to which is the better of the two schools. Each, doubtless, has its excellencies, and each doubtless, will find in the other something that is lacking of good in each. Be proud of your school — Madame and I will not wish to find you other; but be proud in silence. Remember, as the first-comers to this district, we owe a duty to these strangers, and must show them that we, who are proud to think we belong to the Tiernsee, have good manners, and understand what is meant by *noblesse oblige*.

''That is all I have to say to you now. *Abendessen* will be ready in ten minutes' time, and then the juniors will retire to Le Petit Chalet. The middles and seniors may dance for a short time after prayers, and tomorrow we shall commence our work as usual.''

Mademoiselle bowed her head to the girls, and then went out followed by the staff. A babel of sound arose as soon as Miss Durrant, who had come in late, had closed the door behind her.

CHAPTER THREE

The New Arrivals

It was a week after the first day of term that Joey Bettany, glancing out of the dormitory window while she was supposed to be making her bed, saw the signs of arrival. The little lake-steamer which acted as transport on the Tiernsee during the summer months had stopped at Buchau, and was staying there much longer than was to be expected at that season, when visitors were few, and most of those came to Briesau. She promptly informed the others, and they all crowded to the window to look.

"They're just in time to save themselves the walk from Seespitz," said Joey. "The steamers are being docked for the winter on Saturday — Herr August told me so last Saturday. *And* the trains will run for only a week more."

"What a lot of them there seems," remarked Mary Burnett. "How many do you think?"

"'Bout fifty," said Joey. "Wonder what they're like?"

"We'll know that sooner or later," replied the head-girl philosophically. "Come along, you people. Beds ought to be nearly finished by now, and most of you haven't begun."

"Including your sweet self!" retorted Jo, flinging the blankets on her bed.

They were done at last, and while Frieda opened the windows to their widest extent, and Mary and Joey threw up the cubicle curtains, the others ran downstairs to the cloakroom to get ready for their morning walk.

For the first three weeks of this term, the walk came before lessons, and, indeed, they were out of doors as much as possible, for when the snow came, they were frequently prisoners for days together.

The staff had not noticed the arrival of the newcomers, and neither had the middles. Jo, on finding this out, passed along word to her roommates to say nothing, and when Miss Maynard, the Maths mistress, inquired where the seniors would like to go for their walk, Jo, the ever-ready, promptly begged to go round to Buchau, and get the steamer back. "It's going up the lake now," she said, "so by the time we reach Buchau, it will be coming back, and we can go to Seespitz on it. Then it's only fifteen minutes' walk from there if we hurry, and they say winter's coming extra early this year. We sha'n't have many more chances this term, at any rate."

"Very well," agreed Miss Maynard. "Get partners, girls; and remember, no breaking till we are beyond the fence. Are you ready? Mary and Vanna lead, please."

Mary, with her partner, Vanna di Ricci, an Italian girl, set off at a good round pace, and the rest followed in their wake. These walks were always taken rapidly, especially now that the weather was turning colder. Miss Maynard, walking with Sophie Hamel and Lieschen Hoffman, almost had to run to keep up with them. Once past the white fencing that shut off Briesau from the lake-path which led to Seespitz at the lower end of the lake, they broke rank and scattered, though not very widely, for the lake-road at this point was narrow, the wall of the mountainside rising not three yards from the margin of the lake.

Miss Maynard, striding along, with Joey Bettany on one side and Simone Lecoutier on the other, looked what she was — a jolly, frank Englishwoman. Joey, with her high-bred face, was another; little Simone being typically French. In front of them went the others, most of them showing their various races in their faces and bearing, from Vanna of South Italy, to Lieschen Hoffman, who came from one of the North German seaside resorts, and looked it, even in her very English coat and hat of brown material.

At Seespitz, they formed up more regularly till they had

crossed the railway which ran nearly to the ferry-landing, and went past the *Gasthaus* or hotel, where the few remaining visitors looked at them with interest, for this school in the Austrian Tyrol was becoming well known.

As they went round by the path that skirted the water-meadows, they broke ranks once more, and Miss Maynard glanced at her watch. "We have plenty of time, girls," she said, her clear voice reaching the farthest group easily. "Shall we go on to Seehof, and get the boat back to Briesau?"

"Rather!" cried Jo. "Don't you think so, you other people?"

They all agreed, so they went on again, still at the same swift pace, for Seehof was a good way down the eastern shores of the lake, and though the ferry would wait at Scholastika, the little village at the head of the lake, for some minutes, still, there would be no time to waste.

Some of the others fell back and joined the mistress, so Joey and Simone ran on to spread amongst their own friends the news that the new school had arrived, and they might hope to see it as they passed. They were in luck's way, as it happened, for just as they neared the little spit of land known as Buchau, a file of girls could be seen coming down the path to the gate, evidently bound for a walk.

"Though how they *can,* when they've just arrived, I don't know," said Joey.

Later, she learned that they had reached Spärtz, the little market-town at the foot of the mountains, the previous night, and had spent the night in hotels there, so that they had only had the short journey by the mountain-railway that morning. When their Headmistress had suggested that perhaps they would like to have a short walk in order to get some idea of their surroundings before beginning to unpack, they had all agreed eagerly to the idea.

The Chalet girls glanced at them as the two files met — but not too obviously. They were remembering what Mademoiselle

26

had said the night before of upholding the reputation of the Tiernsee. They saw some forty or fifty girls of all ages, from ten to sixteen, who wore coats of saxe-blue, and black velour hats with gold cords round the crowns and little gilded shields in front, on which were stamped what was evidently the school-badge and motto. Their shoes were black, and struck observant Jo as a good deal too light for the rough roads of the district. The Chalet girls wore thick stockings of brown wool when they went for walks at this time of the year, and stout nailed shoes to match.

"That must be the foreign school the Head spoke of," said one of the newcomers when they were past. She made no attempt to lower her voice, and the clear tones carried on the crisp mountain air, so that most of the Chalet girls heard what she said. "They *are* a dowdy-looking crew, aren't they?"

"Is that all of them?" asked another voice. "It *must* be a small school, mustn't it, Elaine?"

After that, they were out of earshot, but the Chalet girls had heard quite enough. Joey, in particular, was furious. "What nerve!" she gasped, when she was sure the new school couldn't hear her. "To talk about us like that!"

"Most likely they thought we shouldn't understand," said Mary sensibly. "They called us a foreign school, so I expect they don't understand that we know English as well as other languages."

"I don't care — it was nerve!" insisted Joey. "If any school here is a foreign school, it's theirs, for they've just come, and we've been here for three years and a term. But it's just what I should have expected from anyone who had anything to do with that awful woman!"

"Jo, if you speak so loudly, Miss Maynard will hear, and then she will be angry," warned Frieda. "There are a good number of them, are there not? Perhaps they will play netball and hockey, and then, as Mademoiselle says, we can have matches against them. I think that will be very nice.''

Joey pulled a face. ''I don't want to play any matches against a set of apes like that, I can assure you. Oh, all right! I'll be quiet now. Mary, is that the boat getting ready to sail for Seehof? 'Cos if it is, we'll have to hurry!''

Mary passed back word that the boat was casting off from St Scholastika, and Miss Maynard promptly bade them run. They all took to their heels and fled, and just reached the landing in time. Luckily, the captain recognized them, and he had held up the little *Kron Prinz Karl* till they reached her. Miss Maynard was last on board, and then the ropes were cast off, and they went off across the lake to Geisalm, the little hamlet before Briesau.

''Did you see the new school, Miss Maynard?'' asked Mary.

''Yes,'' said Miss Maynard. ''And now I know why some of you were so anxious to come this way for your walk!''

Joey flushed. ''It does make a jolly walk,'' she murmured uncertainly.

''It does. But if you had told me your real reason for wanting it, I should have preferred it,'' said the mistress quietly.

''But what do you think of them?'' persisted Mary, partly because she really wanted to know, and partly to change the subject.

''They look quite pleasant girls,'' said Miss Maynard. ''I think they are accustomed to playing games, too.''

''I say!'' Jo had been seized with a new idea, or she would not have drawn the attention of the mistress to herself just yet. ''What will they do for a playing-field? There isn't any room at Buchau; and even if there was, the land all slopes down to the lake, and jolly sharply, too.''

''So it does,'' said Mary. ''What will they do, Miss Maynard, do you think?''

Miss Maynard shook her head. ''I haven't the slightest idea. As you say, it is rather a problem.''

"They may, perhaps, hire a field by the water-meadow," suggested Simone.

"Such a long way to go," objected Jo. "It would take quite twenty minutes to get there; and the water-meadows are often squelchy in bad weather, and take ages to dry up."

"And there's no room at Torteswald, either," put in Marie von Eschenau. "You know how the road comes close up to the mountain-slopes. The only field near them is old Mutter Annchen's on the little alpe, and as her cows live there in the summer, and the upper half of it she uses for hay, there would be no room for games."

"Anyhow, it slopes too," said Deira O'Hagan, a pretty Irish girl, who was second prefect this year. "They'd be getting no games at all for running after the ball when it ran down to the lake."

"Perhaps they will not have games?" suggested Paula von Rothenfels doubtfully.

"It's an *English* school," said Sophie Hamel. "How could they do without?"

"But — but — if they haven't any playing-field, and can't practise, how are they going to play us?" demanded Joey in consternation.

"That remains to be seen," said Miss Maynard. "Here we are. Make haste girls, or half the morning will be gone before we get any work done."

They scrambled down the little gangway that had been thrown across from the tiny landing-stage, and formed up in rank at once — for they were in Briesau, where they had to be very circumspect in their behaviour, since it was the most densely populated part round the lake. When they were ready, Miss Maynard gave the word, and Mary and Vanna led the way along the lake-shore, past the numerous hotels which thronged along the path, and so to their own abode, which was shut in by a high wattled fence. Just as they reached it, another procession

29

of girls came winding past, and they had their second view of the new school. So did their own middles, who came from the valley that leads up to the great Tiern Pass into Germany, and turned the corner of the fence just then. As there were thirty-five of the middles, they made a goodly show, for which Joey felt thankful. These wretched newcomers would see that there were quite as many of the Chalet girls as of themselves, and more, too, for here were the juniors coming along from Seespitz.

The new school certainly stared hard enough when it saw the three columns converging on each other, and all obviously belonging to the same school. The girl who had been addressed as 'Elaine,' even turned round in her interest. The Chalet girls were too well-trained to do so — besides, Miss Maynard was behind, and they would have got into dreadul trouble had they done anything of the sort — but they looked at the wearers of the somehwat 'arty' uniform with quite as much interest, even if it was more controlled.

They had gone past, and turned in at the gate, while the middles and juniors meekly waited for their betters to lead the way, when Elaine's voice was to be heard. "I say! They're quite a decent size after all, aren't they? Wonder if they can play games at all? Some of them looked as though they mightn't be too dud at sport."

"Don't you worry, my dear," laughed another voice. "Foreigners never *can* play games for nuts. As for cricket, I don't suppose they would dare to do anything with a ball that wasn't *soft*!"

Joey, overhearing, and thinking of the brilliant play of their team, was nearly weeping with rage, and Mary looked furious. Nothing was said, however, and the girls entered the house in decorous silence.

But once they were safely indoors, Joey broke loose, and her comments should have made the ears of 'Elaine' and her friends burn. "The fat-headed idiots!" choked Miss Bettany, in the safe seclusion of the prefects' room where they were waiting for Miss Maynard to come to give them a maths lesson. "How *dare* they talk like that about us!"

"Foreigners, indeed!" sniffed Mary.

"I think they are *rude*," was Frieda's contribution.

"We'll show them," announced Deira, pausing in the act of sharpening her pencil.

"Yes; but how?" asked Paula.

"Beat them at games, of course," said Marie from her perch on the table.

"If they haven't a field for practice, how are they going to play us, you cuckoo?" demanded Jo with more point than politeness.

"Cavé — Maynie coming!" hissed Sophie Hamel.

Marie jumped down from her perch and seated herself in her chair, and Deira shut up her pen-knife in a hurry, so that when Miss Maynard entered they were all waiting for her, looking just as seniors ought to look. They dared not do anything but work steadily in her class, and today was no exception to the rule; but underneath they were all seething, and it was fairly evident that *something* was bound to happen soon.

CHAPTER FOUR

The Chalet School Scores

It was impossible for the seniors to keep to themselves what they had heard and seen, and soon it was all over the school that the new school had called them 'foreigners,' and said that they wouldn't play cricket or anything that had a hard ball in it. The tale lost nothing in the telling, especially when Irish Deira and Italian Vanna took a hand, and even the Robin was stirred up to wild fury. "But why is it they have said these things about us, when they don't know us?" she demanded fiercely of Amy Stevens, who had become a middle the previous term. "We are *not* as they say — we are *not*!"

"Cornelia says," began Amy, "that they are a set of pie-faced owls."

Robin nodded her head. "That is true. Me, I will tell them so when I meet them."

"Oh no, you won't!" said a calm voice behind her. "I'm ashamed of you, Amy, to teach the Robin such things!"

Amy turned round to face her elder sister, Margia, the head of the middles. "It wasn't me said it first," she declared defiantly; "but even if it was, it's just what they are!"

"Oh, *that's* all right," said Margia tolerantly. "What isn't all right is the Robin saying that she's going to tell them so. What d'you think Madame would say if she heard you saying that, Robin?"

The Robin's lovely little face flushed. "She — would not be pleased," she murmured.

"Very well, then. You aren't to go round shouting it out, either of you. And if you catch any of the juniors doing it, you tell 'em what I said, Amy," directed Margia firmly. "I won't have it. And if *Mary* caught you at it, there'd be stars all round you, and a prefects' meeting to face." She swaggered off, leaving two rather conscience-stricken little girls behind her, and went to join a meeting of her own compeers.

"Buck up, Margia! We're waiting for you to take the chair," said Evadne Lannis, an American child of her own age.

Margia stalked up to the mistress's desk and took her seat on top of it, and looked round on them. There were twelve of them, making up the entire Fourth. The remaining twenty-two made up the Third, and the twenty-one juniors formed the Second and First forms. There were six in the Sixth form, and eight in the Fifth, making up the school to the number of seventy. It was the thirty-five middles who had most of the wickedness of the school in them though some of the juniors were not far behind, and one or two of the seniors had not yet outgrown their mischief.

"What are we going to do about it?" demanded Evadne, when her chief was settled.

"That's what we're here to find out," said Margia calmly. "Now then, you people — the new creatures at the other side of the lake think we are mutts, and are going round saying so. It's cheek, 'cos they don't know anything about us. And they've only just come — *we've* been here for years! What are we going to do about it? That's what I want to know."

"Let us challenge them to matches in netball," suggested Maria Marani.

"Oh, we'll do that all right," said Margia comfortably. "Deira is writing the challenge at this very moment. But let's do something *more*. They've a good nerve to come like this and walk about as if they'd bought up the whole show."

"Could we have a boat race?" suggested Signa Johansen.

"Too late now. They'd never let us. You know how suddenly storms come up on the lake at this time of the year."

"Wait till the snow comes, and then challenge them to snow-fight us," was the idea of someone else.

But the exigent president of the meeting was not prepared to wait for that. "I want to do something *now*," she said plaintively.

Cornelia Flower, another American child, jumped to her feet. "Let's swear a feud against them," she said.

"Mademoiselle said we weren't to," objected Margia.

"Well, call ourselves the Ku-Klux-Klan, and then it *isn't* a feud," put in Evadne. "It'll be the work of a secret organization."

Margia knew perfectly well that it would mean a feud only under another name, but she easily stifled the voice of her conscience, and nodded. "It seems an idea. What can we do? What did the American Ku-Klux do?"

No one was very sure, not even Evadne and Cornelia. Then the former was seized with a brilliant notion.

"Joey Bettany has some of those awful 'Elsie books.' Let's borrow them — they're American all right, so they're sure to say something about them. Then we'll know where we are."

"Brainwave," said Margia, getting down from her seat.

"Cyrilla, you go and ask Jo to trot them out — but don't tell her why we want them," she added.

"Then what am I to say?" asked Cyrilla Mazirús, a rather shy Hungarian child.

"Oh — just say — well, say that Cornelia has mentioned the Ku-Klux, and you want to know about it, so you thought those books might have all about it. That'll be true enough, 'cos it's what we all think."

Thus primed, Cyrilla went off and proffered her request to a startled Jo, who, on hearing what she wanted, stared at her.

"You odd kid! Oh, you can have them if you want them, but take care of them. I know one of them tells all about the Ku-Klux, but I'm not very sure which it is, so you'd better take the lot, and look through them till you find it. Here you are."

Jo piled nine volumes on Cyrilla's open arms, and sped her on her way, without giving the matter another thought. It was

Saturday, and the rain had poured all day, so she was busy with some work for Christmas; she only concluded that Cyrilla was bored and that was the reason for her sudden thirst for knowledge. Afterwards, she said she could have kicked herself for not taking more notice of it; but then it was too late.

Cyrilla went back to the form-room where the meeting was, and delivered the precious volumes over to Margia, who dealt them round as far as they would go, and ordained that those left out must look over with someone. For a time there was no sound to be heard but the turning of leaves. Then, suddenly, Giovanna Donati uttered a cry of joy. "Here it is, Margia! see!"

Down went the other books and there was a unanimous rush to where she sat, and black, brown, red, and fair heads clustered together over the pages. Yes; there it was.

Margia commandeered the book, and waved them all to their seats. "Sit down, an' I'll read it to you. Then we'll know."

The account of the doings of that far-famed 'Klan' as given in *Elsie's Motherhood* shocked them all.

They were so good and quiet for the rest of the afternoon that the prefects wondered what had happened to them, and Mary even peeped into the room to see what was going on. Her amazement, when she beheld them all sitting round listening eagerly while one of them read aloud to the rest, made her gasp. "Are they going to be ill, do you think?" she asked doubtfully of her own clan after she had told them what she had discovered.

"Nonsense!" said Joey. "It's only a spasm. It won't last long — not with that crowd."

After *Kaffee und Kuchen*, they returned to their amusement, and by the time the bell rang for them to go upstairs and change for the evening, they knew all they wanted about the original Ku-Klux-Klan.

"Only we can't go round beating people or sticking up coffins against their back-doors," said Margia regretfully.

35

"No; but it gives us a general idea of what they did," said Evadne.

"Well, it's dancing for the rest of the evening, so we can't discuss it any more. But some of you be thinking out ways of getting those creatures at the other side of the lake to push off, and we'll talk tomorrow afternoon."

The Sunday was as wet as the previous day, and, since there was no service at the little church, even the Catholics had to stay at home. After *Mittagessen* and the rest which at this period of the year they took on their beds, they once more assembled in their form-room, and discussed the question of what they should do with such vigour and earnestness that they never heard the bell for *Kaffee*, and had to be fetched by an indignant Deira, who rated them soundly for not listening. The next day proved to be fine, though bitterly cold, and they were all sent to wrap up, as soon as they had made their beds, for they were to take a long walk. The wind was in the north, and Mademoiselle knew that with this cold, such a thing meant snow, and once the snow came, no one knew how long it would be before it was fit for them to get out again.

The seniors chose to go up the valley this time, towards the Tiern Pass; the juniors went along the lake-path, and the middles, in charge of Miss Stewart, set off for Seespitz. They had just reached the *Gasthaus*, when they saw the long string of new school coming along the road to meet them. At once Margia passed back word to her faithful followers, and they all prepared to do their best. The grass was soaking here, and the path was narrow. The members of the Chalet School spread out a little, and, walking solemnly two abreast, forced the new-comers to step off the path and on to the wet grass. It was done with innocent faces, and Miss Stewart was too new herself to realize that the girls should have been told to fall into single file, so as to leave room for both sets to pass. As it was, the wearers of the light shoes and stockings got their feet and ankles

36

thoroughly wet, and did not hesitate to say what they thought of the causers of it.

"Rotten bad form!" observed one girl.

"Taking up all the path like that," added another.

"Just shows what these foreign schools are like," put in a third.

Miss Steward was at the end of the 'croc,' so missed all this, for the girls were careful not to comment when they were near her. To do them justice, they were not certain that the other school would understand what they said, or they *might* have held their tongues. As it was the middles understood every word, and were boiling.

Margia turned to Cyrilla, who was her partner, and said in clear and slow French, "What rude girls! Do you not think so?"

"But very rude," responded Cyrilla, following her example. "But perhaps they do not know better manners."

Some, at any rate, of the new school knew enough French to follow, and now *they* were boiling.

Elaine, who seemed to take the lead, turned to her partner. "These girls should be taught better behaviour," she observed in French that was not nearly so good as Margia's and Cyrilla's.

Giovanna Donati overheard them, and promptly spoke to *her* partner. "What terrible French, my dear Signa. Where can they have learnt it? And such *big* girls, too!"

By this time Elaine and the rest were past, but they had heard, and they fumed.

The middles went on joyously. On the whole, they considered that they had scored on points in this encounter. They had to turn when they reached Buchau, for the boats were no longer running. But before they did so, they had passed the new school, and were edified to see on its door the words 'St Scholastika's' painted in gilt letters.

"So that's what they are," said Margia thoughtfully.

"*Neck*!" said Evadne indignantly. "To take *our* saint, when they've only just come!"

"I wonder what they were called before?" said Kitty Burnett, whose chief claim to glory was that she was the head-girl's sister.

"Goodness knows! But it wasn't St Scholastika," said Margia with vim. "I'll bet they never even heard of her before they came here."

They encountered the "Saints," as they unanimously dubbed the new school, just before they reached the narrow path, and both 'crocs' passed with a scornful air.

The middles went to their lessons in high glee, for they considered that, all said and done, they had scored most. This pretty little idea lasted till three o'clock that afternoon, when Mademoiselle Lepâttre came in at the end of their singing lesson, and begged permission of Mr Denny to speak to them.

Mr Denny, a tall gaunt individual, who used the language of an Elizabethan, and wore a Tudor air, courteously left the room at once, and the middles faced an obviously annoyed Head.

"I have had a visitor this afternoon," she began abruptly. "Miss Browne, the Headmistress of St Scholastika's School at Buchau, has come to me to complain that you took up the whole width of the path this morning so that her girls had to step into the wet grass. As they were not wearing shoes and stockings suited to such a thing, many of them had wet feet when they arrived home after their promenade. Margia, you are head of the middles — what have you to say?"

Margia got to her feet at once. "I am sorry, Mademoiselle," she said, "but we met them just where the path is narrowest, and we were further along than they, so we felt *we* ought not to be the ones to turn back, and as they didn't — turn back, I mean — we — er — just kept straight on. There isn't room, as you know, for four people to cross just there — or even three."

"But, my child, why did you not go in single file?" asked Mademoiselle.

Margia looked blank. It was not the thing for her to say that they had not been told to do so, since that might have meant trouble for Miss Stewart. So she remained silent.

"Did not the mistress on duty bid you to do so?" continued Mademoiselle, when she guessed from the silence that she would receive no direct answer.

"She may have done, but — but we didn't hear her," conceded Margia.

"Who was on duty?"

"Miss Stewart," said Margia, giving it up as a bad job.

"Ah! She is, of course, new to us, and would not understand," mused the Head. "But then, Margia, you should have fallen into single file yourselves."

"But *they* didn't, Mademoiselle," said Margia; "and there isn't room for three on that narrow path — really there isn't."

Mademoiselle thought for a moment. "I see. Well, *mes filles,* for the future, you will remember that when you are on that path, and meet the other people, you are to assume single file automatically. In the meanwhile, I shall write to Mademoiselle Browne and explain matters to her, telling her what I have commanded you, and suggesting that she shall bid her girls do the same."

"Yes, Mademoiselle," said Margia.

"And you will remember what I have just told you?"

"Yes, Mademoiselle," came in a chorus.

Mademoiselle nodded, and smiled at them. "Then that is well. You may go, now, to your next lesson."

"So that's that," said Evadne later on at *Kaffee*. "I think *we* win this set, don't you?"

"What *are* you talking about?" asked Joey, who was passing at the moment.

But the middles knew better than to give themselves away to a prefect, even though it was Joey Bettany herself.

CHAPTER FIVE

Further Acts of War

"It's snowing," announced the Robin, with a shiver, as she peeped out of the door, her hand held fast in Joey's.

"You're about right," agreed Joey, after she had looked out at the blizzard that was whirling round the house. "Are you well tied up, honey? Then hold tight, and we'll run for it."

Clinging together, the two made off down the little path that led from the Chalet to Le Petit Chalet, and arrived safely, even though they were both breathless.

Miss Durrant, who was head of the Junior House, took the Robin into her study and made sure that she was quite dry before she sent her to Miss Annersley, who shared the responsibility of the little ones with her, to have *Abendessen*. Then she turned to Joey. "Quite dry, Joey?" she asked. "Let me see your feet."

For answer Joey extended a foot well-booted in wellingtons, and the mistress nodded.

"Good! Get your breath, and then you must hurry back. It's going to be a wild night, I am afraid."

"Dreadful — winter coming so soon," said Jo. "We are only just into October, and the snow shouldn't have come for a month yet."

"Still, it has come, so we must make the best of it," said Miss Durrant.

"Well, I must dash back," said Joey, tying her scarf firmly round her head. "Goodnight, Miss Durrant, and thanks awfully."

Even here, where the high fence and the houses helped to shelter them, the wind was like a fiend, rushing round, and catching her, so that she could scarcely stand when it blew in gusts. The snow was wildly confusing, and if she had not the lighted windows of the Chalet to guide her, she felt that she might actually have lost her way.

"At last, my child!" said Mademoiselle, meeting her at the door.

"It was a business getting across!" panted Jo. "If it goes on at this rate, we shall be snowed up by the morning."

Mademoiselle shivered. "Indeed, I hope not," she said. "Go and change your stockings, Joey, and if your dress is wet, then change that also."

"I'm all right," said Joey, showing her boots; "and my frock is quite dry, too."

Having assured herself of this fact, Mademoiselle sent Joey back to her own tribe, and then sat down to write her letter to Miss Browne. When it was written, she put it on one side to be posted on the morrow, and began a long account of their doings to Madge Russell.

The snow continued all night, but at about eight o'clock the next morning, it grew clearer. The Head of the Chalet School took advantage of that fact, and sent Hansi, the boy-of-all-work, off to the post with all the mail of the school. By ten o'clock the snow was once more whirling madly round the house, and the north wind was shrieking to quote Jo, like a thousand banshees let loose.

"No walk *this* day!" said that young person, looking sadly out of the window of the *Speisesaal* while they were having hot coffee and biscuits in the middle of the morning.

"*And* Herr Anserl can't get here," added Margia, with deep thankfulness. "I don't know a thing about that awful Liszt he gave me last week, and there wouldn't be much of me left if he turned up this afternoon, I can tell you!"

"Well, we must get on with all we can," said Mary. "What about giving out the parts of the Nativity play, and letting people get them down?"

"Good scheme," agreed Deira. "Have you got it though?"

41

"Mercifully, yes. Mademoiselle gave it to me last week before they went back to the Sonnalpe."

"I wonder what Mollie and Dick think of this little effort of the weather's?" mused Jo, "I should think they'll have had all they want of snow by the time this is over."

Frieda laughed. "That does not sound well from you, my Jo, who so loves the snowy weather. Do you remember when we skied that Christmas you stayed with us?"

Jo nodded. "What a topping time we had! And the Christmas tree, and the midnight service in the *Hofkirche*! And all your *Grossmutter's* stories to us! How is she, Frieda?"

Frieda's blue eyes grew troubled. "She is old, *die Grossmutter*, and we dread lest we must spend Christmas without her. Bernhilda says that she must be at her bridal, too. But *you* are all coming for that, Jo: Madame and Dr Jem, and little David. Oh, we must pray God that He may spare us *Grossmutter* for long yet!"

"Oh, I'm sure He will," said Jo, with the same simple faith which Frieda showed.

"We all pray for it," said her friend.

The bell rang just then, summoning them back to lessons which went on steadily till one. Then they put their books away, and went off to wash for *Mittagessen*.

When everyone had finished *Mittagessen*, Mademoiselle rose and anounced that, since it was too bad for them to go out, they would have preparation for the first part of the afternoon; and then the parts for the Christmas play would be given out, and someone would dictate it to them, so that they could copy it out and begin to learn as soon as possible.

This Christmas play was now an established affair, dating from the first Christmas term of the Chalet School, when Madge Russell, then Madge Bettany, had written a charming play. No one knew what this year's was to be, and everyone was longing to hear all about it, so everyone settled down to prep in rather a restless frame of mind. At fifteen hours Miss Annersley entered with Mary Burnett, who carried a bundle of manuscript in her hand. Mary gave the precious play to the mistress, sought a place for herself beside Vanna, and Miss Annersley stood up.

"Our play this year is quite a new one," she said brightly. "It is called *The Guest*, and has parts for everyone."

She gave them the story first — quite a simple one, based on a certain legend of the Black Forest. There, the peasantry hold that, on Christmas Eve, Christ comes again to earth in the form of a human, and wanders about asking for hospitality. The peasant of the Schwarzwald keeps the door on the latch on that night, and, if He should appear, a place is laid for Him at the table, and there is food waiting for the Heavenly Guest. Madge's play told of the Coming of Christ as a little ragged Child, who tried in the city to find shelter for the night. But all of no avail, so He left the city and went into the country, and so came to a rude hut, where a charcoal-burner and his family were partaking of supper. When the little Child tapped at the door and asked for shelter, the poor father opened it and bade Him welcome, with the words that have been handed down among the folk of that part for generations: "Come, Lord Jesus; be our Guest." At once, a heavenly chorus arose, and angels appeared to the poor family, singing of God, who came down to earth as a Baby to save mankind. Interspersed with the modern scenes, were scenes from the Christmas Story.

Parts were given next. Marie van Eschenau was the Virgin — that was understood. Mary Burnett had the part of the peasant father, with Vanna di Ricci for the mother. St Joseph was to be played by Sophie Hamel; and Deira O'Hagan, with her dark beauty, was to be the wealthy city lady, with Simone Lecoutier, Bianca di Ferrara, Margia Stevens, and Irma von Rothenfels as her children. Seven of the middles and juniors would be the children of the charcoal-burner; and Paula von Rothenfels was the inn-keeper who had no room for the poor Strangers who came to the inn at Bethlehem. To Joey Bettany fell the part of the Archangel Gabriel; and the Robin was to be the Child, Frieda Mensch and Evadne Lannis were the Archangels Michael and Raphael; and the rest were angels, herdsmen 'keeping watch over their flocks by night,' the three kings from the Orient, serving men and maids at the inn, the servants of the city folk, and the little shepherdess who could find nothing to give to the little King, born in a manger, till Gabriel showed her a bank covered with roses — Christmas-roses — for her gift.

"And the carols," said Miss Annersley, "will be chosen by Mr Denny later on. Now take down your parts."

They worked hard, and got a third of the play taken down before Rosa, one of the maids at the Chalet, rang the bell to summon them to their coffee and cakes.

Evadne said, "Say! Guess we'll have to invite *them*!"

"Invite whom?" asked Joey, staring.

"The little Saints, of course."

There was consternation at this suggestion.

"Goodness! I hope not!" said Jo with most un-angelic vim.

"But, Evadne! What makes you think that?" demanded Marie.

"Don't we always ask the folk round the lake? And how can we cut them out?" asked Evadne.

"What a ghastly idea!" said Margia.

"Evvy's right, all the same," said Jo gloomily, shaking her black head. "You all know what Madame is."

"After they sneaked to their beastly Head! Not me!" retorted Margia.

"Sneaked to their Head? What about?" demanded Mary from the coffee-urn.

"'Bout us making them take the grass by Seespitz," explained Margia succintly.

"When was this? I've heard nothing about it!"

Between them, Margia, Evadne, Cyrilla, and Giovanna told the story of their meeting and its consequences, while Mary

44

frowned more and more as they went on. "I'm ashamed of the lot of you," she said sharply, when finally they came to an end.

"But Mary, it wasn't *our* fault!" protested Cornelia Flower.

"You should have gone into single file *at once*," said Mary. "You know the rule perfectly well, and it was playing it down on Miss Stewart when she didn't. I didn't think you'd do such a thing!"

"But — look here," put in Jo, "has Mademoiselle done as she said? 'Cos if so, I know she hasn't had any reply. And they're right in one way Mary. It wouldn't have made a lot of difference if they *had* got into single file when the Saints didn't. Of course, they knew jolly well what they ought to do, and, as you say, they played it pretty low down on Miss Stewart when they didn't. But still, I don't think we can blame them altogether. It was six of one and half a dozen of the other, if you ask me."

At that point, someone came to say that Cornelia Flower was to go to the study, as Mademoiselle wished to see her at once. She was gone some time, and when she came back the rest were curled up round the stove, listening to a story Joey Bettany was telling them. Into this peaceful group Cornelia burst, with flushed face and eyes bright with anger.

"Say!" she exploded. "That mean rubbernecked clam over there says that our girls were entirely to blame for what happened the other day, and she's been spouting at Mademoiselle about her girls being so good and well-behaved, an' she can't say as much for ours; an' for the future, will she tell us that when the two schools meet, ours are to go back and make room for hers!"

This speech created a great sensation.

"*What* did you say?" demanded Deira O'Hagan, getting up quickly — Mary and some of the others had gone to do work by themselves. "Are you sure, Cornelia?"

"*Sure*?" Cornelia nearly spluttered in her wrath. "You bet your bonehead I'm sure!"

"But — how rude!" commented Frieda Mensch.

"She is a person of no breeding," said Marie von Eschenau, "or she would never have said such a thing."

"I vote we shove their precious saints into the ditch the next time we meet. Guess *I*'m game for a little thing of that kind!" This was, of course, Evadne.

"Evvy, you ass, shut up!" said Joey in a troubled voice. "Look here, Cornelia, word of honour, did she say all that?"

"Rather!"

"But — how did you hear?" asked Marie suddenly.

"'Cos I was there," said Cornelia simply.

"But — you don't mean that that woman came and said all those things to Mademoiselle — and on a night like this?" And Joey glanced out of the window, where the snow could still be seen whirling round and round in a giddy dance.

For the first time Cornelia looked uncomfortable. "N-no. Not exactly," she stammered.

"Not exactly?" Jo was on her like a flash. "What do you mean?"

"It — it was over the 'phone," explained Cornelia, becoming the colour of beetroot.

There was a gasp.

"Do you mean to say you *listened* while Mademoiselle held a private conversation with someone else over the 'phone?" demanded Joey, standing very upright and looking very much of a prefect.

Cornelia was no coward, however. She stood straight, too, and her big blue eyes met Joey's angry black ones without flinching. "Yes, I did. She knew I was there, I guess, 'cos she heard me come in. I stood to one side to wait till she'd finished, and I heard all that was said, 'cos Mademoiselle kept repeating it — sort as if she couldn't believe her ears, you know."

"Well, you should have spoken," insisted Jo. "I'm sure she never meant this to come to us — it's the last thing she'd have wanted. And now, you can trot right back to the study and tell her what you've just told us. As for you others, you're all going to give me your word of honour that you won't tell anyone else. Understand?''

With Joey looking like that there was nothing for it but to promise, and the story was checked at once; while a crest-fallen Cornelia wended her dreary way back to the study and owned up to Mademoiselle that she had heard all that had been said over the telephone and had repeated it to the others.

Mademoiselle, who had been too much taken aback by Miss Browne's unexpected way of meeting with her pleasant note to see that anyone was in the study besides herself was rather shocked to find how much had gone to the girls. She feared that it would not mend matters, nor help to quell the feeling she instinctively knew was growing up between the two schools. So she scolded Cornelia soundly for her behaviour, and told her that if such a thing should occur again she would lose her privileges as a middle for a week.

Cornelia was very humble, and apologised meekly; but the mischief was done. Hereafter, the Chalet School and St Scholastika's were to be at daggers drawn.

CHAPTER SIX

A Little Hockey

Two days later the snow stopped, and it froze hard. Jo Bettany, waking early on the Wednesday morning, sat up in bed to look out, and found that the window-panes were covered with wonderful ferns and leaves and stars, and that she couldn't see through them at all. With a grunt, she lay down again, for it was too early to switch on the light and read. As she lay watching, her mind went to the feud which had lost nothing of strength during the two days they had been imprisoned in the house. "What can we do about it?" she thought. "Madge would be furious if she knew."

It was only too evident that Miss Browne had put an end to any attempts at friendliness that might have been made, and, knowing her sister's wishes, Jo felt unhappy about it. "I've a good mind to write to Grizel and Juliet about it," she thought. "*And* Gisela. I wish I could get hold of Gisela, but there's no chance of her coming down in this weather, and I'm positive they won't let me go to the Sonnalpe till half-term — and not then if this continues."

The shaking of her curtains roused her from her musing. She sat up, and switched on her electric torch. "Who's there?" she asked in cautiously-lowered tones.

"Mary!" replied tones equally as low. "May I come in?" Mary slipped in and, sat on the bed.

"What do you want?" asked the hostess somewhat inhospitably.

"It's this wretched business with the Saints," said Mary. "Jo, what are we to do about it?"

"Can't do anything that I can see," replied Joey. "We can squelch the kids if they show signs of being blatantly rude. But that's about all."

"I wish we could manage to put a complete end to the feeling," said Mary. "Madame would hate it, and those little asses, Evadne and Cornelia, are going about talking about 'newcomers,' and being horribly snobbish."

A rustle of bed-clothes near at hand warned them that someone was waking up, and the next moment Frieda Mensch asked sleepily in her own language, "What time is it, Joey?"

Jo burrowed under the pillow of her watch. "Ten-past seven," she said. "The bell will ring in a minute."

"Then I'll go to my own cubie," said Mary.

The other members of the dormitory began to wake up.

"Is it snowing still?" asked Simone.

"Can't see," said Jo, "but I shouldn't think so, for the windows are covered with frost-patterns."

"Oh, good! Then we can go out at last," said Marie. "There rings the bell — now we must get up."

There were six separate bumps as six people tumbled out of bed, and then a rush of feet as the first four made for the bathroom. By a quarter to eight everyone was dressed.

They turned back their curtains, stripped their beds, and opened the windows to put in the woods that let in enough air to air the rooms thoroughly. During the cold weather it was impossible to open windows as they did in summer, for the cold in the Tyrol is intense, exceeding anything dreamed of in England.

Downstairs, they were greeted by the middles with demands to know whether they would have their walks today.

"Three days in the house," grumbled Margia. "It's enough to try the patience of a saint!"

"P'r'aps we'll have games," suggested Evadne. "D'you think so, Jo?"

Joey shook her head, and declined to commit herself.

"Well, Deira, then?" Evadne turned hopefully to Deira who had just come downstairs. "Do you think we'll have games today?"

"Not regularly," said Deira. "But we might take hockey-sticks when we go out, and knock a ball about as we go. There couldn't be any harm in that."

So after breakfast, when they were bundling up, ready for the long outing, Deira and Mary went to Mademoiselle and got permission for middles and seniors to take sticks and balls with them when they went, provided they did not try to play along the narrow path between the lake and the mountains. They promised, and nine o'clock saw them setting forth, every girl well wrapped up, with a shawl fastened crosswise over her chest as the Tiernsee people did at this time of year, and each carrying a hockey-stick. They wore thick socks whose tops were rolled above their stout boots. The attire was not beautiful, but it was warm, and they ran little chance of taking cold, thus garbed.

" 'Croc' till we reach the grassy part near Seespitz, girls," said Miss Maynard, who was in charge of the seniors. "After that, you can break ranks and use your sticks. We are staying out for at least a couple of hours; for, unless I'm very much mistaken, the snow will come down again by the afternoon."

She glanced at the sky as she spoke. It hung, dark and heavy, close to the mountain-peaks, and foretold further storms before long. In its frame of driven whiteness the lake showed the black of the first ice, and every tree branch was laden with snow. Up the valley the black trunks of the trees stood out with startling distinctness against the purity of the snow, and the chalets and hotels round the lakes showed drifts against the walls, while the roofs were deeply covered. The crisp air stung the warm colour to the cheeks of the girls, and in it sounds rang with a sharpness that was surprising. Over in the field the juniors were to be seen, racing about after each other, while their shouts came clearly to the seniors and middles who were dividing at the gates of the school — the middles going off up the valley, while the seniors made for the lake-path.

They walked decorously enough till they were past the narrow path, then, as the way broadened to the grassy land rolling out on either side of Seespitz, Deira flung the ball across to Mary and they were off.

It was good fun, even though tackling of any kind was forbidden, and they might only pass to one another. Faces glowed and eyes sparkled as they grew warm with the exertion, and laughed and shouted. Their nailed boots gave them a good grip on the frozen surface, and all had good balance and poise.

By degrees they came to the water-meadows, where the grass was hidden by the snow, though rifts here and there told of frozen water beneath. Under their flying feet the thin ice crackled and snapped, and they enjoyed themselves thoroughly.

They were startled out of their absorption in their game by the sound of feet and voices, and, looking up, they saw the Saints coming along, slipping and sliding as they did so.

"Oh, how silly!" cried Deira to Jo, as she saw them. "They haven't had their boots nailed!"

"Don't they look like hens on hot bricks?" said Jo, with a chuckle, as one girl slid and grasped at another, who almost went down in the effort to keep herself erect and support her friend at the same time.

Their clear voices carried on the still air, and the Saints were furious.

"Just look at those girls!" said one, a big girl of fifteen or so. "Don't they look sights, bundled up like that?"

"Yes — just like villagers out for a frolic," replied another. Miss Maynard, who had heard all the speeches, frowned sharply, but could do nothing. The Chalet girls had not meant to be rude. Their remarks were only for the benefit of each other. The Saints were obviously talking at their foes — for such, it was evident, the two schools considered each other.

Deira, at that moment, shot the ball to Paula, who muffled it and let it pass. It went hurtling along in the direction of the Saints' 'croc,' and seemed likely to go bounding over the borders of the lake on to the ice. It was very shallow there, as they knew, but even so, it seemed unlikely that the young ice would stand having a hockey-ball bouncing on it without breaking. The Chalet girls watched it with horror.

Then someone stepped out of the ranks of the Saints, set a booted leg in the way of the flying missile, and stopped it neatly.

"Well stopped!" shrieked Jo. "Jolly well stopped!"

The girl who had stopped it, stooped down and picked it up, flinging it back to Mary with a steady throw.

Deira, as games-prefect, called "Thanks very much!" and then the Saints' mistress came up, and, at sight of her, Miss Maynard stopped. "Why, Gertrude!" she exclaimed in surprise.

The lady looked. Then she came swiftly across the ground. "Mollie Maynard!" she cried. "Why, what are you doing here?"

"The same as you, I imagine — teaching. I am senior mistress at the Chalet School."

"Oh, I'm only matron at St Scholastika's," replied the other. "Are these your girls? I've heard about them. I have a crow to pluck with them, you know. I've had three people in sick-room as a result of getting their feet wet the other day.

Miss Maynard laughed. 'I heard about it. But your girls were equally to blame with ours, you know. That path is too narrow for more than two people to pass at once. Generally, the mistress in charge tells the girls to fall into single file. But the middles were out with a new mistress that day, and she didn't under-stand. Neither, I gather, did yours. But we mustn't let the girls stand about like this on such a day."

"No; it's dreadfully cold," agreed her friend. 'But how *do* you people keep on your feet as you do!"

"Nailed boots," explained Miss Maynard. "See!" and she held up one foot to show the special nails driven into the soles and heels, and round the toes, to give them a grip on a slippery surface. "These are climbing-boots, and we all wear them for weather like this. The sooner your girls get them, the better."

"I agree. As it is, we have to move so slowly that I daren't keep them out for very long, in case they catch cold. So we must move on now."

Meanwhile the girls had been looking at each other. Mary, with a feeling of responsibility, moved across to where a couple of big girls stood shivering. "It's cold, isn't it?" she said cordially. "May I introduce myself? I am Mary Burnett, head-girl at the Chalet School. And these are Joey Bettany, Deira O'Hagan, Marie von Eschenau, and Frieda Mensch," introducing those who stood near.

The girls stared in unfriendly manner. "Oh," said the elder. "This is Doris Potts, and I'm Elaine Gilling. I'm captain of St Scholastika's."

"Were you always St Scholastika's?" asked Joey with interest, pronouncing the name as the Tyroleans do, with the 'S-c-h' soft.

Doris, who seemed a more pleasant girl than Elaine, shook her head. "Oh no. We were St Margaret's in England. But when we came here, the Fawn thought it would be a good idea to adopt a local saint, so she pitched on the old saint at the end of the lake."

"Play games?" asked Deira.

"Of course," said Elaine. "We had a jolly good hockey-team before we came here. But it won't be much good practising in this place where there isn't anyone to play against."

"Oh, but that's where you're after making a mistake!" cried Deira. "We play, for one; and it often happens that a school comes up here for the climbs, and they play too. We have played netball frequently with them, and, once or twice, hockey. But, at least, we are here all the time, and we play a good deal."

"But we had an excellent team, and played some stiff matches in England," said Elaine. "Of course, our Second Eleven might be about your standard, but that won't be much use to *us*."

53

Mary laid a hand on Deira's arm, only just in time, for the Irish girl had a hot temper and was given to saying what she thought.

But Jo was too far away for the head-girl to get near, and she ran Deira a good second. On this occasion she stared at Elaine, and then said, "Oh, I don't suppose your Second team would find it much fun — ours would wipe up the earth with them. We played a team of ladies last year which had five county players in it, and drew with them too."

Mary drew a sigh of relief that the remarks had been so gentle. There was never any saying what Jo might remark.

Doris giggled. "Oh, we aren't so dusty," she said. "But look here, we shan't have much time for talking. Matron will be shunting us on again in a minute. Tell us about your school. Did you come from England, too?"

"Not exactly," said Jo. "At least, my sister who started the school and I did, and she and Mademoiselle Lepâttre began it. Then my sister married, and Mademoiselle is carrying it on. We began with me and Grizel Cochrane and some Austrian girls came too. Then we grew and grew, and now we're seventy, and we've a good many old girls as well."

"How long have you been here, then?" asked another girl who had just come up.

"Four years," said Mary.

At this point, the two ladies finished their conversation, and the matron of St Scholastika's — they learnt later that her name was Miss Rider — called her girls together, and Miss Maynard sent hers back to their game.

The Saints returned home while the Chalet girls were just turning back from the road to Seehof, along which they had chased their ball almost to Seehof itself. They could see the long double file of girls marching in at the door of the new chalet, though they were still some distance away.

"Poor lambs!" said Joey. "And we've got more than an hour yet!"

"Have you, though?" said Miss Maynard's voice just behind her. "You've nothing of the kind, as it happens. Pick up that ball, Deira, and get into the rank, you people. I don't like the look of those clouds, and we're going to set off home as hard as we can pelt, or we may be caught in a blizzard."

She pointed to some peculiar, yellowish clouds that were coming up in the north as she spoke, and the girls needed no further warning. They set off at a long loping run which they could keep up easily for some time.

They rounded the head of the lake, and went on along the path till they came to the narrow part. There they had to slow down, for there was not room for running with any degree of safety.

There was a curious hush over everything, and the sky was a colour that made imaginative Jo shiver when she looked at it. "I wish to goodness Maynie would let us hurry," she said apprehensively to her partner, Simone Lecoutier.

"So do I," said Simone. "I do not like this stillness."

They had passed the narrow part, and almost reached the fence, when a long low moan came out of the north.

"Keep together, girls!" called Miss Maynard. "Take your partner's hand! Now then, all *run*!"

Clinging to each other, they set off, but even as they reached the gate in the fence the wind was on them, blowing in fierce gusts that nearly took them off their feet. The snow had not yet come, but Miss Maynard, experienced in the weather of a Tyrolean winter, knew that it was not far behind. She was right. Almost immediately after the gust it came, not lightly-dancing flakes, but with a cruel whirling that turned them giddy and made it impossible to see more than a yard in front of them.

"Keep together!" she shouted at the top of her voice, but the wind snatched away the sound, and she could not be sure that they had heard. Running as fast as she could, she managed to get to the head of the file, and caught Mary's hand in hers.

"Deira, turn and hold the next girl's!" she shouted. "Tell them to pass it on."

This time she was heard, and they all linked up. Then, with the mistress leading, they went cautiously along, keeping to the path as well as they could. Miss Maynard had taken Mary's hockey-stick and was feeling in front at every step, for she dreaded leading them all into the lake. Luckily, they did not do that, though in the general hurly-burly they went right past the Chalet and came up to the Stephanie, one of the hotels open for the winter, where the lights, gleaming through the snow from the windows, warned them that they had gone astray.

It took them half an hour to get back to the Chalet palings after that, and it wasn't till her groping hand felt them that Miss Maynard breathed freely. Then she did relax. Feeling their way in the blinding storm, they managed to reach the gate, and once inside it they were safe, for the path leading to the door was fenced in with a low fence that, in summer was covered with creeping-roses. The door was open, and Mademoiselle was standing there, ready to welcome them, with Matron in the background.

They stumbled wearily up the path and over the threshold, into the passage which had never seemed so safe or beautiful before. Joey was done, and dropped as she got in, and Simone Lecoutier and Marie von Eschenau were not in much better case; but the others, once they had got their breath, were all right. The three frailer members of the party were sent to hot baths and to bed, where they spent the rest of the day. The others had the baths and then went down to their form-rooms, where they sat by the fire, resting and recovering themselves from what had been a most unexpected adventure.

"It's been a thrill," said Jo that night, when the others had come up to bed and they were discussing it. "Also, we've got to know some of the Saints. What do you think of them, anyone?"

"Not much," was the reply.

"Some of them don't seem bad," she said thoughtfully. "But that Elaine girl struck me as being rather an ass. And I don't suppose they'll deign to play us at hockey, so we may as well give it up as a bad job. But it would do them a lot of good if they did, and we beat them."

"No one has ever called you conceited, Jo!" mocked Mary.

Jo sat up in bed — in direct defiance of Matron's orders. "I'm not! But I'd *love* to take that Elaine creature down a peg or two!" she said fervently.

CHAPTER SEVEN

Marooned

Winter had begun in real earnest now, and for nearly a fortnight there was very little going out. Every now and then the snow would cease for an hour or so; and it made no matter what the girls were doing — on the instant everything was dropped and they were told to get into out-door things and sent out to run about while they could. The only rule was that they were to stay near the house, in case of the snow coming on again suddenly and badly.

At length the long storm came to an end, and one morning they were all turned out after *Früstück*, and sent to get ready for a long walk.

"Middles and seniors together," said Mademoiselle. "The juniors will go for their own little walk, and this afternoon we shall begin with the rehearsal for the play. Mr Denny will come from the Villa Adalbert for carols at four o'clock, and to-morrow, if the weather continues fine, Herr Anserl will come up from Spärtz for piano lessons. After singing, we will have our *Kaffee und Kuchen,* and then, since the moon is at full to-night, the middles and seniors will take a moonlight walk — if it stays fine."

There was a cheer at this, for they were rarely out at night during the winter, and the thought of a walk over the crisp snow, was too delightful to be greeted with silence.

After that, they were dismissed to put on their things, and when they were ready they set off, this time in the direction of Geisal.

"Oh, are we going near the dripping rock?" cried Jo. "How topping!"

"Will it be frozen?" demanded Margia. They were walking

anyhow. "Won't it look lovely, with long spikes of ice dripping down?"

They went along, past the Kron Prinz Karl, past the narrow path, and the little rustic bridge over the stream which now lay dead under the ice, beyond the meadow that only six weeks ago had been so flowery, and so to the far fence. From there the path led beneath the snow-laden trees of a pine-wood, till they reached rocks, along which they had to go carefully, since they were slippery, and though the Tiernsee was now frozen over hard, and there were one or two figures already skimming over its surface on skates, yet it was so deep here that Mademoiselle was still a little anxious.

"Wonder what the Saints are doing?" said Joey suddenly to Mary, as they negotiated a stiff little climb.

"Probably going either to Seehof, or else the eternal way to Seespitz," said Mary. "They never seem to get anywhere else."

"They don't live at the really interesting side of the lake, do they?" said Margia.

"No; that's us," declared Jo, with a grin. "Look out, Margia — there's a nasty bit here! You'll have to make a long stride of it. Up she goes! I say, Mary, we'd better stay here, I think, and help all the kids across. It's rather a chasm, isn't it?"

"It is," agreed Mary. "I'm sure there wasn't a rift like this when we were here in the summer."

"It's a real abyss, Mademoiselle,' cried Joey, as the Head came near.

Miss Wilson, who was with her, looked anxious suddenly. "What are you talking about, Jo?" she asked.

"This crack," explained Joey. "D'you remember when we were here in the summer, there was a little one? Well, something's happened, and it's hefty now. Look!"

Miss Wilson looked, and her grave face grew graver still "All right, Joey," she said shortly. "Go on now. I can help Mademoiselle across."

Joey went on, and raced after Mary, who had got a little in advance while she had been talking to the mistress.

"What an age you've been!" was the greeting she received.

"Bill was yarning about the cleft," explained Jo. "Come on, let's get in front."

They set off at a good round pace, and Miss Wilson's gravity faded from Jo's memory as they neared the dripping rock and finally reached it.

It was a tall rock, standing out from the mountainside, and obviously part of an alm. A stream that watered the alm found its outlet here. During the summer months it dripped down into the lake but now, when the frost had come in dead earnest, the water hung in long beautiful icicles that had assumed all kinds of graceful or fantastic shapes. The pale wintry sun gleamed on, making them shimmer with rainbow hues, and the sight was a wonderful one.

The girls stood round, exclaiming and admiring for some minutes. But they were not permitted to stand for any length of time. It was bitterly cold, and, even wrapped up as they were, they were risking chills. Mademoiselle moved them on, and they went on towards Geisalm.

"Wish we had our skates here," said Jo. "Wouldn't it be gorgeous to skate home from Geisalm?"

"It would. But we shouldn't be allowed to do it, anyway," said Mary. "There are springs between here and Briesau, and ice is never safe where there are springs."

"Listen!" interrupted Marie at this moment. "I can hear voices behind us."

They listened, and sure enough, on the clear air, they could hear the sound of merry voices.

"It must be the Saints," decided Simone.

She had barely finished when there was a sudden scream, and everyone started violently.

"An accident!" cried Miss Wilson, turning round and making for the place at top speed.

Some of the elder girls went after her; Mademoiselle held back the rest, saying imperatively, "No! There is no need for all to go."

She kept them with her, and meantime, Miss Wilson with Joey, Mary, Frieda, and Vanna was hastening back along the narrow rocky path. They passed the dripping rock, and still sped on, for the sound of voices and confusion was becoming clearer with every step. At length they turned a curve in the road, and there they saw a good half of St Scholastika's School all crowded round the rift they had crossed such a short while ago.

Miss Wilson hurried up, saying, "Is there an accident? Let me help."

At once the girls drew back, and then she — and her own four — saw what, as Joey later stated, sent their hearts into their mouths. The friable rock, strained by the frost and the great weight on it, had broken off, the rift was now quite literally a chasm some six feet across, and all the upper portion of the Chalet School, as well as some thirty or so of St Scholastika's, were imprisoned in the Geisalm part of the lake-shore!

Miss Wilson and her girls stood stock-still as they took this in. Miss Wilson was not really so surprised, for Jo's words had told her that the place was likely to break away sooner or later. As for the Saints, they stood about wringing their hands and exclaiming with horror. Then a tall gaunt lady, looking anything but beautiful in a heavy tweed coat, with a scarlet woollen scarf tied round her neck and a red cap pulled well down over her ears, pushed forward amid the girls on the safe side of the chasm and saluted Miss Wilson.

"Miss — er — I don't know your name, I'm afraid, but I am Miss Browne, the Headmistress of St Scholastika's; and I suppose that you are one of the staff of the Chalet School. As you see, the rock has given way here, and several of my girls are on your side. I wish to know what can be done about getting them safely back here."

61

"My name is Wilson," said the Geography mistress of the Chalet School. "*All* our girls except the juniors are over here, and I wish to know how we are any of us going to get back."

"Well, we can't get round the other way," remarked Joey in a detached manner. "The path is all broken up near the other end of the lake, and it isn't safe at the best of times, let alone now!"

"Oh!" exclaimed Elaine, who was on the wrong side of the chasm. "Couldn't we skate?"

For reply, Miss Wilson pointed down to the ice below where the rock had fallen. It showed long cracks that were extending farther out. "There are springs about here," she said. "I'm afraid the ice won't bear."

The Saints looked aghast, and one or two of the smaller ones seemed about to burst into tears. Miss Browne looked wildly round her, and then turned back to Miss Wilson. "Well, have you anything to suggest?"

"Not at the moment," said Miss Wilson calmly. "I don't know if we can get through the woods at the back of Geisalm to the mountain-slopes; or even if success in that way would mean that we could climb to the alm, and so get down to the Tiern Pass. I have never tried to do it; nor have I heard of anyone else doing it, but — well, Joey?"

"Oh, Miss Wilson," cried Joey, "there must be a way down somehow, because there's a little tiny village on the alm above — you can see it from the Bärenbad. But I don't know if they ever come this way, or if they go down to the Pass. But I know it's there."

Miss Wilson looked thoughtful. She turned and examined the ground around, and then pulled back the girls who were standing nearest the edge, flinging out her arm and crying, "Get back girls, at once!"

The urgency in her voice compelled them to instant obedience, and it was as well, for even as they went there was an ominous cracking, then a roar, and more rocks began to slide down to

62

the ice on the lake, causing the cracks to extend farther and making the ice shudder and groan.

"I don't know how far this is going to be affected!" called the mistress when there was comparative silence again. "Not much farther on this side, I think. But I advise you to go back a little. The frost has made all this part intensely friable, and any undue weight may set it slipping again."

At the words, Miss Browne gave a yell and moved backwards a good two feet. At the same time there came footsteps from the Geisalm direction, and then the remainder of the upper part of the Chalet School appeared, headed by Mademoiselle, who was looking rather distraught, though her face lightened when she saw that the Geography mistress and the four girls were safe. Miss Wilson went to her and explained matters to her as quickly as she could, while the girls themselves stood round, deeply thrilled by the adventure.

Miss Browne, meanwhile, was bewailing her fate in having chosen to take this walk. She could do nothing but wait till she heard what the mistresses on the other side of that wide gap — it was now more than eight feet across — were going to do. Finally, Miss Wilson came as near to the edge as she dared and called for her. "Miss Browne! We are going to send someone to Geisalm to find out what the people there think will be our best plan. In the meantime, I advise you to make the girls move about. So long as they don't come any nearer the edge than they are at present I think it will be quite safe. Vanna and Frieda, I want you to run to the *Gasthaus* at Geishalm, and ask for Herr Schenke. Bring him here, and, Frieda, on the way tell him what has happened."

The two nodded and set off, and Mademoiselle and Miss Wilson set all the girls on their side, Saints as well as Chaletians, to running briskly along the path to the edge of the great fan of loose shale that has to be crossed before you reach the little wooded triangle that leads to the Geisalm.

Miss Browne followed their example on her side by making what girls she had left move about to keep themselves warm. Then, after about twenty minutes had passed, Vanna and Frieda put in an appearance, one on either side of a little dark man with bright quick-glancing eyes. He said he did not advise them to attempt to bridge the gulf. The ice was as impossible. Even the hard frost they had had would not be sufficient at this time of year to make it safe for them to attempt to cross it. The one thing they could do was to go through the pine-wood behind his *Gasthaus*, climb to the alm where stood the little village of which Joey had spoken, and so cross down to the Tiern Pass. It would mean a long walk, but it was comparatively safe, and the only thing to be done under the circumstances.

Then he added to his information by offering that his wife should get some sort of a meal for the girls before they set off. It would be four o'clock before they reached Briesau, and the young ladies would be exhausted if they went without food for that length of time. It was not the season, so they had not much that they *could* offer the gracious ladies — only bread and bowls of coffee.

After a long consultation with Miss Browne, who was very much upset at the idea of losing sight of her girls for so long, it was decided to do as he suggested. Miss Browne was to take her remnant home, calling at the Chalet on her way back to tell them where the others were, and Mademoiselle and Miss Wilson would bring all the others over the alm to the Tiern Pass, and so to the Chalet School. Miss Browne was to be at the Chalet at six, for it was certain that the girls would be too tired after their long scramble to set out on the additional four miles to Buchau straight away. Indeed, Miss Wilson was privately prepared for keeping most of the Saints that night; though she only spoke of it when the two parties had separated, and the seventy odd girls in their charge were going on in advance in a long 'croc,' with Mary Burnett and Elaine leading, as the two head-girls of the respective schools.

"I expect it," said Mademoiselle, in reply to Miss Wilson's observation. "But is there no one with a cart to whom we could send a message to meet us at the foot of the pass?"

"If only Mr Bettany had been still here!" sighed Miss Wilson.

But Dick Bettany had moved to Innsbruck when Jem Russell had gone back finally to the Sonnalpe, so there was no possibility of getting to him.

"There is August Stein," suggested Mademoiselle, with a brightening face. "He has a horse and a hay-cart. It would be better than nothing, and we could send the most weary of the girls home in it."

"Ring up the Chalet when we get to the *Gasthaus*, and ask Matron to send to him, then," said Miss Wilson. "He might know one or two other people who would come too, and then all the girls could ride. Do you think we shall be able to eat at this tiny village of Jo's? Because, if not, we had better see if Herr Schenke can give us anything to take with us."

They reached the *Gasthaus* in safety, to find Frau Schenke bustling round importantly. She had already lit the big stove in the *Speisesaal*, and coffee was boiling in the kitchen. Luckily, she had made a baking of bread only the previous day, so there would be plenty for the hungry girls, and she promised that they might have some to take with them, all ready sliced up. Milk she was sure they could get at Mechthau, the little village on the alpe, for most of the people kept cows.

The girls sat down to a plain but hearty meal of new rye-break broken into bowls of hot milky coffee, well sweetened with coarse sugar, and enjoyed it. The sharp air had given them all fine appetites, and they had been out in it for nearly two hours. When it was over, they got up, and thanked their kind hosts — who refused to take a share of the little money that the two parties had with them, saying that they knew the Chalet people would pay as soon as they could get the money to them, and that they would need what they had to buy milk at Mechthau. Bearing parcels of rye-bread cut into slices, they set off through the little pine-wood at the back of the *Gasthaus*, escorted by Herr Schenke, who showed them the easiest way up the mountain-slope, and who bade them "Godspeed" before he turned and went back to his home.

CHAPTER EIGHT

The Long, Long Trail

Mademoiselle had arranged the girls in groups of threes, for some of the younger middles were a good deal "younger," and would need help. She was thankful to see that the Saints had good climbing boots, Miss Ryder having insisted on it that day after she had got her girls home from the brief walk they had been able to take. Most of them had alpenstocks as well, and she hoped that they would manage to reach Briesau by the afternoon without any accidents.

The girls, warmed by the coffee and rested and refreshed, looked on the whole affair as rather a joke, and set off gaily. Luckily, Miss Wilson was an Alpinist, and she promptly called back those who had set off at top speed. "You can't climb at that rate," she said severely. "You must keep to a steady pace. Remember to bend your knees well. You will save yourselves a little as you go. Mary Burnett, will you and Amy and — Elaine, isn't it? — keep ahead. You are to set the pace."

"Yes, Miss Wilson," said Mary obediently, and, with little Amy Stevens between them, the two big girls went off.

Jo Bettany, with Cornelia Flower hanging on to her arm, was paired off with a dark pretty girl, who introduced herself as Gipsy Carson; Frieda undertook Kitty Burnett, and had made friends with a slim Scottish girl, Elspeth Macdonald; Simone, with Yvette Mercier was partnered by Doris Potts; and Deira had fraternised with another Irish girl, Maureen Donovan. The others were duly sorted out, and then they set off, Mademoiselle and Miss Wilson bringing up the rear with Giovanna Rincini and Marta von Eisengau, two people who were apt to lag behind on all occasions.

"How d'you like the Tiernsee?" asked Joey politely of her

new acquaintance, as they struggled up the long slope which was the first part of their journey.

"It is very beautiful," replied Gipsy with equal politeness.

"Guess it is," put in Cornelia. "I'll tell the world I've never seen anything to beat it."

"But it's very cold, isn't it?" said Gipsy.

"Oh, only in winter. You wait until the summer," Joey told her. "You'll find it hot enough then!"

"Where was your school in England?" asked Cornelia.

"On the south coast, not far from Worthing," said Gipsy. "I live in London," she added.

"We used to live in Devonshire," said Joey, "and I don't know London much."

They came to a curve in the path at this moment, and Jo paused to look out across the black lake in its setting of white snow, with the great snow-crowned mountains rising beyond and the pale blue of the late October sky above. The sun was still shining, and the snow sparkled gaily under its rays.

"That is very beautiful," said Gipsy softly.

"Glorious," said Jo.

But there was no time for dreaming over the loveliness of the scene, so they went on. The path was becoming steadily steeper, and progress was growing slower as the unaccustomed Saints panted and struggled on. There was no question of being cold. Everyone was boiling hot with the exertion. The Chaletians gave a helping hand where it was necessary, but it was easy for none of them, now that the ground was hard and slippery. The younger girls especially found it hard.

After a while everyone was too breathless to talk, and the merry chatter, with which they had begun their journey, died down. Even Jo felt it would be a great deal wiser to save her breath, and went on in comparative silence.

At length they came to a place where the path forked, and here Mary stopped. "I'm not too sure which way Herr Schenke said we had to go," she said. "We must wait till the others come. Bill will be sure to know."

"I think it was the left he said," said Elaine.

"I thought it was the right myself," returned Mary. "But in any case, we ought not to get too far ahead."

"Oh, rubbish!"

"Lean against me, Amy," said Mary, quietly ignoring the rude rejoinder. "No, you can't sit down, but you can get your breath, and I'll hold you up a bit."

Elaine made one to two tentative steps in the direction of the left fork. "I'm convinced this is the right way," she said. "Yes; it must be. See how easy it is."

"Lots of the paths look easy enough at first," returned Mary. "Farther on they may become goat-tracks. Don't go, Elaine. We can't afford to lose any time going after people who have taken the wrong road."

By this time Joey and Frieda with their partners had come up to the place.

"Well, which way?" queried Jo.

"I'm not sure. We'd better wait for Bill, I think."

"I'm positive he said to the left," put in Elaine. "It's shorter, too, because it's in the Briesau direction. If you go the other way, it's the opposite way altogether."

"That's nothing to go on," Jo assured her. "The way these paths twist and turn, it never means anything. I rather think he said the right, but I wouldn't swear to it, 'cos I wasn't listening. Do you know, Gipsy?"

Gipsy shook her head. "I think it was the right; but like you I can't be sure. Mary is right, Elaine, I know. we ought to wait till the mistresses come."

Some of the others joined them now, and when Miss Wilson came up to them, there was quite a little crowd waiting for her. "To the right, girls," she said briskly. "Then when the path forks again, go to the left. You'll have to climb carefully. Herr

Schenke said that it was full of tree-roots and there are some boulders as well. Don't try to hurry. We are doing very nicely, and once we reach the alpe, it'll be easy going for a while.''

Elaine frowned heavily as she came back and joined Mary and Amy. She was a very proud girl, who hated to be in the wrong about anything. As she was more than year older than any of the other Saints, they all looked up to her and followed her in everything. Mary was busy easing the way for Amy as much as possible, and there was no talk at all between the two leaders.

Joey, Gipsy, and Cornelia went on with only an occasional remark. Jo was beginning to like Gipsy Carson. She seemed a jolly girl, with plenty of common-sense about her, and her dark prettiness was very attractive. Shy Frieda was with a girl almost as shy as herself. Elspeth Macdonald had only had one term at school prior to the move to the Tyrol and, before that, she had lived in the Highlands rarely seeing anyone but her own people. She thought Frieda Mensch very pretty and "nice," but the pair had little to say to each other, and bent their energies to helping Kitty Burnett, who found the way far from easy.

Deira and Maureen were quite different. Both were Irish; both came from County Cork, and both had the same out-of-school interests. When they had wind enough, they chattered gaily together, and got on very well indeed. In between times they lent a hand to Maureen's little sister Bride, who was far too young to be making such a journey.

Simone, with Yvette to help her, managed several remarks to Doris, who chattered amiably enough, but privately wished she had been put with people of her own race.

The path now led steeply up the mountainside, and the frost made it difficult going. The little ones had to be helped a good deal, and all things considered, Miss Wilson was beginning to wish that they had found some other solution to the difficulty, when a cry from Mary and Elaine informed her that they had reached the alpe.

"Here at last!" called Mary. "Mind the last two yards or so, Miss Wilson; they're horribly slippery! We'd better stand by to give a hand to the middles, hadn't we?"

"Please, Mary!" called Miss Wilson in reply.

The two big girls stood to help up the tired junior-middles when they reached the last bit of the way. Slippery it certainly was, and, but for the strong hands extended to pull them up, it is safe to say that one or two at least of the younger girls could never have negotiated it. As it was, little Bride Donovan and Kitty Burnett had almost to be lifted up to the alpe; but at last everyone was standing on level ground once more, and sundry people were rubbing their legs and complaining of aches and pains.

Miss Wilson allowed no standing about, however. "Come along, girls! It's no use complaining; you must just grin and bear it. We are past the worst now, I hope. The village is near here, I believe. We shall get some hot milk, and you will eat your bread and have a short rest."

They went on, Miss Wilson leading now, for there were thick pine-woods on this alpe, which was much larger than any they had hitherto seen, and no village appeared at first.

"I don't believe there's such a thing!" grumbled Elaine at length. "Your Miss Wilson isn't going in any definite direction, as she would if she knew it was there. It's my belief that she's just scouting round to get the quickest way down without giving us any rest at all. Grown-ups always think it's better not to tell you outright!"

"Miss Wilson isn't like that!" cried Mary indignantly. "And I think you'd better hold your tongue about her, if that's all you can find to say!"

Elaine glanced at Mary. "Oh! Keen on her, are you? Sorry — didn't know, of course!"

Her tone implied more than her words did, and Mary had to bite her lips very hard to keep from replying. Luckily, at

71

this moment, the spire of the church, rising out of a large begilded ball, as is the custom in the Tyrol, appeared through the trees, and the argument ceased. They hurried on, and soon came to the village.

A very tiny village it was — not much more than a hamlet, with a dozen or so chalets clustered round the little church, while, at a little distance, were to be seen one or two larger houses. Behind it rose the mountain, and in front there was the dark pine-wood, with the snow glittering in the light of the pale sunlight that was beginning to die away now, for it was three o'clock in the afternoon, and by four the sun would have set. Two or three men were standing about, wearing rough coats wrapped round them, and with the inevitable china-bowled pipes in their mouths. A woman, with a shawl hugged closely round her, came out of the first of the chalets, and looked at them in amazement.

Jo went forward and spoke to her. Yes; the gracious ladies might have milk; cheese, also. Had they come far? From Geisalm? *Herrgott*! What a climb for weather like this! And they were doubtless of the school of which even up here in Mechthau they had heard?

Joey explained that they were two schools, and further told of the mishap to the lake-path. The woman nodded her head understandingly. Then she opened her door and ushered them all in.

The room they entered was of considerable size, but was stiflingly hot. A huge stove stood in one corner, and a cheery fire burnt in it. The windows were shut tightly, and, what was more, had material of some kind fastened over the joinings. A table stood in the middle of the floor, and on it was crowded a variety of things including a large pan of milk, yellow with cream. There were one or two stools and a couple of chairs. In a corner, opposite the stove, was a built-in bed on which their hostess invited the smaller people to sit. Then she picked

72

up the pan and went through a door at the back of the room and they were left to find what seats they could or sit on the floor, which was not too clean. Miss Wilson insisted on having the door opened − for seventy girls and two grown-ups made the atmosphere stifling.

The milk came, very hot, rather smoky, and with a curious flavour of onions, cheese and wood-ash. Still, it was very welcome, and when they had all taken it in turns to drink out of the big mugs in which it was served, and had eaten their bread, they felt better.

Miss Wilson paid for the milk and called to the girls to get their partners and fall into rank outside. Most of them did as they were told, but it was discovered that Bride, Kitty, Amy and Giovanni Rincini had all fallen asleep. The heat of the room and the warm milk had sent them off and it was with difficulty that they were aroused. Even then, they staggered forth still drowsy, and it was some minutes before they woke up properly.

Along the alpe they all went, very tired and most of them very stiff. The rest had been a very welcome one, but they had to pay for it and some of the more unaccustomed Saints, grumbled loudly as they went. The Chaletians, as became people who had been in the country for some time, and who were Guides, said nothing, but set their teeth and went at it.

The alpe was very long, or so it seemed, but at length they reached the path that led down to the Tiern Pass, and then the Saints found that, hard as climbing *up* had been, climbing *down* was considerably worse. They slipped and they slid, and they clung wildly to whatever was handiest − generally the nearest Chaletian − and the noise they made with their screams and shrieks as they progressed downwards must have caused a good deal of amusement to the people of Mechthau, who had followed to the edge of the alpe to see the last of them.

''And they say how easy it is to go downhill!'' panted Gipsy, at one pause. ''Whoever said that first was a silly ass. Well, if once I get to the level I never intend to leave it again, and so I warn you!''

''The pass isn't exactly the lever,'' said Jo cheerfully, as she gripped Cornelia's arm to steady her over a rough bit. ''And this is *nothing* to the way Elisaveta and I came one day!''

''Which is Elisaveta?'' asked Gipsy.

''Not here now,'' said Joey.

''She's Crown Princess of Belsornia'', put in Cornelia who knew the whole story to which Jo had just referred.

''I *say*!'' Gipsy was suitably excited. ''Did you really have a Crown Princess at the Chalet School?''

''She wasn't then,'' said Joey. ''Her father was it — Crown Prince I mean; but her grandfather has died since, and he's King now so Elisaveta is Crown Princess, and that is why she had to leave school, so that she could be crowned.''

''That was Madame's last term as Head'' said Cornelia mournfully. ''I always feel kind of lost because I wasn't here then.''

''Who's Madame?''

''Jo's sister that started the school.''

''But where's she now?''

''On the Sonnalpe with Jem'' said Joey. ''They've been married fifteen months, and I have a nephew — David.''

Gipsy had come to a bit that needed care, so she had no breath for chattering for a minute or two.

They negotiated the difficult bit in safety, and finally reached the Pass — all very weary, all very stiff, but no one hurt beyond a few scratches and bruises. It was dark by the time they got there, and they had to go slowly and carefully, but finally they reached the end and there were the hay-carts, into which they all scrambled thankfully. They were driven back to the Chalet School where the Chaletians climbed out and staggered up the path, while the Saints remained, for the men had agreed to drive them direct to Buchau.

After a large supper, over which as Joey remarked later, they all 'did themselves proud,' they were sent off to bed where they rolled in, and most of them were asleep in five minutes and never stirred till noon the next day. Only in the prefects' dormitory was there any conversation.

"What d'you think of them Joey?" asked Mary as she pulled off her stockings.

"Who — the Saints? I rather like the girl I was with — Gipsy Someone-or-other. She struck me as being a jolly girl. I'll tell you one I *don't* like, any more that I've ever done since I first met her, and that's Elaine."

Mary tossed her stocking into a corner. "I don't like her either," she said. "But what I meant was what is your general impression of them?"

"Oh, they might be worse," said Joey who was now in her pyjamas and preparing to say her prayers. "They've an *ass* of a Head though."

"Well, they can't help that," said Mary. "I think Deira had better see about sending them a hockey challenge soon."

Jo dropped on her knees by the side of her bed with a little suppressed scream. "Ouf! I'm stiff! Moving will be torture to-morrow! Yes; I suppose she might as well. On the whole, I think it'll be rather fun having them here. Now I'm going to say my prayers so don't talk."

Silence prevailed for the next few minutes while the others followed her example. When the last girl was in bed Frieda, the quiet, uplifted her voice, just before Mary as head-girl, turned off the light. "So there will be no feud," she said "and I am glad of it my Jo."

Jo, well buried beneath her bed-clothes, grunted drowsily and the next moment the dormitory was in darkness.

CHAPTER NINE

Elaine Speaks Her Mind

The next day the Saints all woke up very stiff and sore after their long walk. They had had no previous experience of mountaineering to prepare them for what would follow, and they moaned and groaned when the relentless bell called them out of bed at nine o'clock.

"Rotten luck!" said Elaine as she dragged herself up into a sitting position. "O-o-oh! I feel as if I'd been beaten all over!"

"I'm a mass of bruises," declared Doris with a groan. "I kept waking up in the night and trying the other side to see if it was any easier, but it was *worse*!"

"Gipsy looks pretty rotten," said the head-girl of the Saints with a glance at Gipsy Carson. She was not a strong girl, and the climbing and walking had strained her severely.

Elspeth Macdonald better accustomed to that sort of thing than the others, got up and went over to Gipsy's bed. "You do look ill Gipsy," she said in her soft Highland voice. "Hadn't you better lie still and let me fetch Matron to see you?"

"Oh I'll be all right when I'm up" said Gipsy cautiously manoeuvring herself into a sitting position. "Don't fuss Elspeth! And if you go to Matron, I'll never forgive you!"

Elspeth limped back to her own bed and sat on it preparatory to pull on her stockings, while the others crawled out of bed and, by dint of much labour, got into their clothes. Hair-brushing was an ordeal with aching shoulders and arms but at length they were all ready and hobbled downstairs where about half the school were assembled. Many of the younger girls were still in bed, and several of those up looked fitter for the same place. Miss Browne was fussing about ejaculating and exclaiming and calling Matron first to this girl and then to that. Matron, worried

76

and busy was irritable and the rest of the staff looked troubled.

Gipsy was sent straight back to bed, with orders to stay there till she was given permission to get up; and she was not the only one. When, finally St Scholastika's sat down to breakfast only thirty-seven of them were at the table. The rest were all between the sheets, and Matron with two of the staff were busy with breakfasts. Lessons were a mere farce for no one felt inclined to take the smallest interest in them, and even those who had been spared the walk were far too excited to pay much attention to what they were taught.

At St Scholastika's there were five mistresses besides the Head and Matron. Miss Soames taught mathematics; Miss Anderson took English subjects, including history and geography; Mademoiselle Berne took French and German; Miss Elliott was the music mistress; and Miss Phipps was the junior-mistress, and had charge of a form of ten little girls whose ages varied from ten to twelve. Miss Browne taught Scripture and some English; and such subjects as drawing, physical training, singing, and games were divided amongst the staff. When break came Elaine Gilling who, as head-girl, always took the lead, gathered her own special friends together and carried them off to what was known as the senior common-room.

Among the crowd she had collected were Doris Potts, Maureen Donovan, two sisters — Winnie and Irene Silksworth; a pretty feather-headed child of fifteen called Maisie Gomn; Vera Smithers, a girl whose people had made a fortune during the war, and who adored Elaine because her father was a baronet — a more appalling little snob than Vera was never found in any school — and Hilda Wilmot a dreamy, artistic girl, who was rarely more than half-awake to all that went on about her, and who was in the habit of letting Elaine do her thinking for her about ordinary life in a way that was bad for both of them.

Miss Browne, goaded thereto by the various reports of the mistresses, had announced that break would last for an hour after which there would be one more lesson, and then they would be free till dinner-time. Elaine therefore determined to make the most of her time. Her stiffness and bruises had kept her awake during the night, and she had spent the long hours in turning over in her mind all that she had learnt about the Chalet School during the previous day. She had taken a dislike to Mary, whose downrightness had upset her; and she had hated Joey Bettany from their first moment of meeting. Apart from this, she possessed the insular type of mind, and she was inclined to look down on a school the majority of whose numbers was made up of what she designated in her own mind as "rotten foreigners." So she had formed a plan, and it was to discuss this that she had summoned her satellites in this way.

"What do you want Elaine?" asked Doris when they were all assembled. "Buck up and tell us for it's jolly cold here and I want to go and get warm at the fire."

"Don't be silly!" said Elaine sharply. "If you care more for your comfort than your school, go of course. But if you do, well, I shall know what to think of you — and so will the rest of us."

Doris was a well-meaning girl but she had not much brain, and she meekly gave in and pulled her jersey round her with a shiver and a longing look at the fire in the open fireplace. Miss Browne had not seen fit to have the great stoves to be found in most continental houses and the rooms were less evenly warm in consequence.

"I want you," began Elaine, "to form a league with me."

"What sort of a league?" asked Winnie Silksworth.

"A league to have nothing to do with that other wretched school," said Elaine. "Listen! I'm sure they look down on us just because they've been here longer than we have. You should have heard the head-girl of theirs talking yesterday! She might have been the king from the airs she put on! And a good many of the others were horribly patronising too! They kept saying things like, 'Of course when you've been here longer you'll

78

know all about that'; and 'Oh don't you know *that*?' as if we were a set of idiots and they were college professors at the very least! I hate that sort of thing — especially when it comes from foreigners who aren't anywhere to be compared with *us*, and I'm not going to put up with it. I vote we form a league to have nothing to do with them, and to show them that they are absolute nobodies. What do you think?''

"How are you going to set about showing them that they are nobodies?" asked Maureen Donovan practically. "If you're going to have nothing to do with them that means that you won't play them at matches; so what are you going to do?"

"That's true," said Doris. "If we took them on at hockey and netball, I daresay it would be quite easy to beat them. They have so few English girls that they must have to make up their teams with the foreigners, and we must be pounds better than they are 'cos we've played nearly all our lives, and foreigners are never much to write home about at games, unless it's tennis or something mild like that. But if we're not going to play them at matches we can't do it."

"And besides," put in Maisie, "didn't the Fawn say that she was going to arrange with their Head about matches?"

"We can refuse to play them," said Elaine.

"Of course we can!" cried Vera rushing to the rescue of her adored Elaine. "If we all say that we're not going to have a thing to do with them at matches, or anything else, that plan will soon fizzle out. Most of us are in the Hockey Eleven, and as for netball the kids will do as we tell them."

Maureen got up. "I think you and Elaine are asses!" she said tersely. "I won't be joining you in this. And if that's all you want to say, Elaine I'm going over to the fire. You can count me out!" With this she strolled over to the fire leaving Elaine startled and dismayed.

"Silly ass!" exclaimed Vera who was the first to recover. "Never mind Elaine. We're well rid of her. Tell us your plans and don't bother about her! *We* aren't going to be traitors to you." Her last word was chosen with intent. She had guessed at a wavering in Doris, and perhaps the Silksworths, and she had no mind to stick to an unpopular minority. At the same time, she knew that many of the girls in the school had no great love for her, and she hated the thought of being left out of things. Her words turned the scale in Elaine's favour, and those left to the head-girl settled more firmly round her.

"Go on," said Winnie. "Tell us what we are to do."

"You are to have nothing to do with the Chalet girls," said Elaine pulling herself together. "No one is to speak to any of them and no one is even to see them if we meet when we are out. Remember, if it hadn't been for their idiotic idea of that awful climb yesterday, we shouldn't all be as dead tired and stiff as we are today. If that mistress of theirs had had any sense, she'd have managed to make arrangements to have the gap bridged. But she had to show off with her wonderful girls, and so we all have to suffer for it today. I haven't had time to think of anything special yet, but I soon will; and then we'll show them! The Fawn told me that that Joey Bettany's father, or brother, or something was most rude to her when she spoke to them on first coming here, and said that as they had the Chalet School at the Tiernsee, they didn't want any other. The cheek of it! We've got to back up the Fawn, and let them see that they don't own the earth or even the whole Tiernsee, as they evidently think!"

Now what Miss Browne had said to Elaine — was that she feared they would not find it easy to make friends with the Chalet School. They had seemed to resent her suggestion — made before she knew that Joey Bettany was already a member there, and that it partly belonged to her sister — that Jo should come to St Scholastika's. It was of course, a mistake to have said anything at all about it, but Miss Browne was in the habit of confiding a good deal to her head-girl. Elaine had twisted it round in her own mind and now delivered her own version to her friends, rousing them all to boiling-point.

"We'll show them!" was the general attitude of the meeting, and when the majority of the school had heard what the seniors had to say, they agreed, to the smallest junior. Of the whole fifty-three of them, only six stood out — amongst them Maureen Donovan who said it was all nonsense; Gipsy Carson who agreed with Maureen; Bride Donovan, who followed her sister in everything and three juniors who were Bride's special chums and who, with her, were known as The Quartette. Otherwise, the Saints made up their minds that they would ignore the Chalet School on all possible occasions and, somehow or other, would show them that there were other schools much better than they!

Having done so much it came as a shock to Elaine when three days later, Miss Browne announced that on the Sunday all the members of St Scholastika's would go to church in the big hall at the Chalet. "As I think some of you already know," she said, "Mrs Russell, who is sister of one of the prefects at the Chalet School, founded it, and still has a considerable interest in it. Her husband is the Dr James Russell of the sanatorium on the Sonnalpe, and recently a young clergyman of the Church of England has come with his wife, who is ill. He is staying there to be with her and has offered to take Sunday services, when it is possible, for all those at the Chalet School who are members of the Church of England. Mademoiselle Lepâttre, the Head of the Chalet School, has written to me asking if I should like you to join. I have accepted the offer and on Sunday if it is fine you will all go to the Chalet School for eleven o'clock service. The clergyman, Mr Eastley, has very kindly offered to come down on the Saturday once a month, and hold Eucharist for the sake of those girls who are confirmed. So will you all be ready by ten-fifteen on Sunday to walk to the Chalet School. Dinner will be at one-thirty."

The rest of the week passed quietly and Sunday was a brilliantly fine day. Snow had fallen heavily on the Saturday, but had cleared off during the night and a hard frost had made it delightful for walking. They went round the lake and through the gate of the Chalet School. They did not go to the Chalet itself; instead they were met by Mary Burnett, in Sunday hat and coat and gloves, and led round the house to a large room built on at the side. Here already seated in the chairs at one side, were those of the Chalet girls who were not Roman Catholics — some twenty or so — and four of the staff. Margia Stevens was at the piano to play for the hymns and psalms, and Miss Maynard was waiting at the door to direct them to their seats. The service was not a long one, and they had plenty of hymns, and Mr Eastley preached a short and simple sermon on making the most of one's opportunities. A collection was taken in aid of the poor of the district, for, as Mr Eastley said when announcing the object it was their duty to do what they could to relieve the terrible want that oppressed the Tiernsee people in winter. A final hymn was sung, and then all knelt for the blessing. When it was over, Margia played softly till the clergyman had retired and then they all streamed out.

The Chalet girls, who were rather in the position of hostesses engaged their guests in talk at once.

"Do you like our little chapel?" asked Joey eagerly of Elaine. "It was only built and dedicated during the summer holidays. It *is* nice, isn't it, to have our own little chapel?"

Elaine looked at her scornfully and turned away.

Mary, speaking to Doris Potts, got no better treatment and most of the others fared the same. The Chaletians were aghast. They couldn't think what they could have done to deserve this.

Luckily, it was too cold for standing about, and Miss Browne and her staff hurried the Saints into rank and marched them off, after thanking Mademoiselle Lepâttre, who appeared for a few minutes, for her kindness in making this arrangement for them.

Then everyone went in for *Mittagessen*, and as Mr Eastley was there, they had to be on their best behaviour. But once they were set free to do as they liked for the afternoon, great was the discussion among them of the bad behaviour of most of the Saints.

Margia Stevens promptly revived the old idea of the Ku-Klux-Klan, which was received with acclamation by most of her circle and they spent a very enjoyable time planning various affairs to teach the Saints good manners. The prefects were not quite so violent, but they were very indignant.

They finally left the subject, and turned to the much more agreeable one of the play.

Meantime the Saints walked home, most of them with a virtuous feeling of having done their modest best to show the Chaletians how lowly they had rated them. Only Gipsy and Maureen felt ashamed of the exhibition of bad manners on the part of their school. They talked it over as they walked home together and decided that it was time something was done about it.

That something they did after dinner, when they both talked themselves hoarse all in vain. Elaine and her coterie only laughed at them, and then turned on them and called them traitors to their own school.

"It's you are the traitors, then!" cried Maureen. "Giving the school a name for bad manners! That's what you're doing."

"Rats!" said Elaine. "All we're doing is showing those beastly foreigners how decent English girls regard them. They started it first with that wretched Joey Bettany's relatives. It's you who are traitors and — and blacklegs! You aren't attempting to back up the Fawn, though I've *told* you how that man treated her!"

"I don't believe any of Joey Bettany's relatives would behave as you *say* they did!" retorted Gipsy. "She's a jolly nice girl from all I've seen of her and I don't care if it does make you mad my saying so."

Things were at a dead-lock. Elaine refused to move from the attitude she had taken up. Gipsy and Maureen vowed that the rest of the school were idiots, and finally they marched off, followed by the faithful Quartette, who found a fearful joy in being "agin the Government" in this way.

CHAPTER TEN

The Chalet Guides

For the early part of the week both schools were too busy with lessons and everyday work to bother much with each other. When they went for walks which happened on the only two days when it didn't snow, the Saints persuaded the mistresses in charge to go along the Seehof road. The Chaletians on one occasion went up the valley to Lautebach, the little hamlet just below the mouth of the pass, and on the other, the juniors were kept to play in the field with the younger middles, while all those of thirteen or over took the mountain-path that leads to Spärtz and went down as far as the saw-mill which is worked by water-power. In the summer this path is bordered by a stream that leaps and dashes down its bed in headlong fashion. Now it was frozen over, and a deep silence lay on all.

Saturday came, bright and clear, and on this occasion Miss Maynard, captain of the Guide Company, saw fit to have a march-out.

They were very glad. Lately, Guide meetings had been spent largely in work for the Christmas-tree which they gave to all the children round about on the last Saturday of term. The weather had kept them indoors so much that they had been able to do no open-air work, so this was an unexpected treat.

"We won't go to Geisalm this time," said Miss Maynard, laughing. "I think we'll march round the lake to Seehof and then come back. I don't want to tire you too much. Herr Braun came over to see Mademoiselle early this morning. He skated over." She paused, and a sigh of deep joy rose. This meant that the ice was safe for them at last and that skating would begin.

"When may *we* skate, Miss Maynard?" asked Joey.

"If the weather holds, this afternoon," replied the captain.

A loud cheer arose at this news.

"All of us?" asked the Robin, who in her Brownie uniform was standing very straight.

Yes, *mein Vöglein*. Everyone of you may skate a little," replied Miss Maynard with a smile at the school-baby.

"And now, to work! Company — *'shun*! Brownies — right *turn*! Forward — *march*!"

The Brownies marched smartly away to their Brown Owl, Miss Durrant, and she took them off, for they were not to go on the Seehof route, that being entirely too far for their small legs.

"Guides — left *turn*! Forward — *march*!"

Led by Mary Burnett, the senior patrol-leader, they marched smartly out of the hall and set off along the road.

The French have their *Eclaireuses*, the French Guides, but here in the heart of the North Tyrol there had been no such thing till the Chalet School had started its company to which nearly everyone belonged.

It was a glorious day for marching — cold, with a 'bite' in the air that stung the colour to their faces and made them glad to keep moving. The sunshine of late October set afire a million frost jewels in the snow, and the black lake gave added loveliness to its whiteness. The sky was a pale-blue, flecked with tiny white clouds, though to the north the clouds appeared heavier, and gave evidence of the fact that there was more snow to come. The mountains looked magnificent in their spotless winter robes, and the black trunks of the pine-trees in the forests that clothed some of the lower slopes showed in sharp silhouettes and cast long blue shadows across the blanched landscape. The Guides marched in silence at first but presently Miss Maynard sent back a command and they broke into the delightful swing and rhythm of the Guides' song.

They rounded the lake and turned into the Seehof road still singing. An old peasant woman who was coming slowly along on her way to Spärtz, paused to look at them and smile. They all knew her — she was the old apple-woman who in the summer, sat by the roadside with two big baskets of fruit before her and a pile of paper 'pokes,' in which she sold her fruit. They smiled to her as they passed, and she called after them the pretty Tyrolean greeting "*Grüss Gott!*" Then she turned and went on, and the Guides, their song finished, marched in silence for a little.

Presently Miss Maynard began the Harrow song, 'Forty Years on' and they all took it up, their clear voices ringing through the frosty air. After that they sang 'Men of Harlech' and this brought them up to the gate of St Scholastika.

The Saints were getting ready for their walk when the song floated across to them and those of them who were quite ready rushed to the nearest window to see what was happening. Elaine and Gipsy were among them and they stood on tiptoe to see over the heads of the smaller girls.

"They've got *Guides!*" exclaimed Elaine, bitterness in her voice. "Oh, it's *too* bad!"

Gipsy said nothing. Everyone in the school knew that Elaine was longing to be a Guide. Unfortunately, Miss Browne objected to the movement. That the Chaletians should have a Guide company now seemed to Elaine to crown the rest of their iniquities.

She was a peculiar girl in some ways. She was given to brooding over things till trifles assumed the proportions of mountains, and she was fond of putting constructions on the most innocent words and actions that no one else could possibly see. She had imagined so long that she had a grievance against the Chalet School that now she had succeeded in convincing herself that it was so. Now she turned away, an angry bitter feeling rising in her.

Gipsy looked after her, a peculiar expression on her face. She, too, longed to be a Guide, but she had felt that, when they came to this part of the world they would never meet such a thing. It was a tremendous surprise to her to find that the Chalet School had a company at all.

The Saints took their partners and 'croc-ed' for their walk along the Seehof road, many of them in bitterness of spirit. As a whole the school wanted Guides and only the Head's determined stand against the movement blocked the way. They would not even have lacked for Guiders, for Miss Soames and Miss Elliott had both been Guides for many years.

Among the very few girls at St Scholastika's who had no interest in the movement was Vera Smithers. She did not usually say so for she knew better than to antagonise Elaine by so doing. Now, however, she felt pretty safe. So when the Saints met the Chaletians as the latter were marching back from Seehof she elevated her nose at them and remarked in loud tones to her partner Winnie Silksworth "Oh, look at the good little soldier-girls in blue!"

The Guides heard, as they were meant to do, and were furious. Cornelia turned purple, but Evadne Lannis, who was marching beside her, gripped her arm warning her to control herself.

Vera went on in high feather at the thought of having — as she considered — scored off the rival school. She told Elaine about it later on adding airily "If *that's* the sort of people who are Guides I can quite understand the Fawn saying she won't have them in the school! We don't want to be mixed up with people like that. Why, you couldn't know who they are!"

"Vera Smithers!" cried Gipsy Carson who had overheard her. "Of all the rotten little snobs I ever met, I think you're one of the worst!"

"Your opinion wasn't asked," returned Vera.

"I daresay — but you're getting it, all the same! As for who those girls are, I can tell you they've had better-class girls in that school than have ever been in *this*! Since you're so interested in that kind of thing, you may like to learn that they have had a princess there — the Crown Princess of Belsornia. So there!''

''I don't believe it!'' said Vera flatly. ''Who told you so?''

''Joey Bettany, and that child they call 'Cornelia'!''

''Oh well, you've only *their* word for it!''

''Oh, it's true enough,'' said Elaine carelessly. ''That head-girl of theirs, Mary Somebody-or-other, told me about her. But she's only been Crown Princess for a few months.''

In spite of herself, Vera looked impressed. She did love a title so!

''And that awfully pretty girl, Marie von Eschenau,'' went on Gipsy. ''Her father's a Count. And Margia Stevens's father is Charles Stevens, the author of *Glorious Prague*. And there are heaps of others. So the less *you* have to say about 'better-class girls' the more you'll shine!''

By this time they were all getting heated, and, as the argument went on, their voices rose higher and higher, till finally the noise attracted the Headmistress, who came to inquire what was the matter. The scene she found in the senior common-room so shocked her that she promptly announced her intention of punishing them by forbidding skating that afternoon. As they had all been looking forward to it, this was a dreadful blow; and Elaine, furious at being deprived of her favourite sport, became openly impertinent, with the result that she received a reprimand that made her flush.

''You forget yourself, Elaine!'' said Miss Browne with unwanted severity to her head-girl. ''How dare you speak to me like that? You may lose a conduct mark, and if I have to complain again of your manner, I shall send you to bed. Let me have no more of it.''

· Elaine raged at being spoken to like this before everyone, and she set it down as one more count against the Chalet School.

The sight of the juniors going off joyously with Miss Anderson, Miss Elliott, and Matron to essay their first attempts at skating was not soothing to the ruffled feelings of the seniors and middles, and even quiet Elspeth Macdonald lifted up her voice to say that she wished Miss Browne had chosen some other punishment.

The Saints were unable to practise opposite their own school, for the lake is very deep thereabouts, and Miss Browne had been warned about it. They were taken up to the Seespitz end, where figures were circling gaily backwards and forwards, and their seniors and middles could not see them. What they *could* see, however, was the entire Chalet School on the ice before its grounds, having a good time.

Most of the girls kept near the shore, but presently three girls, with hands interlinked, shot out towards the centre of the lake, where some bold people were disporting themselves, and went flying off towards Seehof.

"Wonder who they are?" said Gipsy.

"Let me see," said Maureen, pushing her to one side. "Oh — yes! It is Joey Bettany, and Marie von Eschenau — and that quiet one they call Frieda. Aren't they having the good time of it?" she added wistfully.

"Topping!" said Gipsy, with a sigh.

"Oh well, I expect the ice will last a few days yet," said Doris Potts, joining them at the window. "Didn't one of those girls say that it would go on for weeks and weeks?"

"She did — that little quiet one — Frieda What's-her-name," replied Gipsy promptly.

"But sure, what's the good of that *now*?" sighed Maureen. "It isn't *tomorrow* I want to be skating, but *today*!"

"Then you'll have to want!" said Gipsy.

But Maureen, always ready for mischief, was not stopped so easily. "What's the matter with getting out after tea and going, then?" she asked. "Sure it's dark 'twill be then, and who's to know where we are? Don't they leave us alone till seven? And what's to hinder us getting dressed, and finding our skates and going on the ice for half an hour or so? We needn't go far — just about here. Round the corner beyond the old tree would be a fine convenient spot, and no one to see us!''

Now this is where Elaine should have put her foot down at once. But Elaine was feeling sore at all that had happened, and she did nothing of the sort. Instead, she pretended to be buried in her book and never looked up. "Serve the old Fawn right," she thought, as she deliberately shut her ears to what was going on. "It may teach her to let us alone another time, perhaps!''

Elspeth Macdonald protested, and Gipsy asked Maureen not to be such an ass. But what they said had little effect on the wild Irish girl. Most of the others were smarting at the loss of the afternoon's fun, and Maureen soon found followers in plenty. Finding that Gipsy, Elspeth, and one or two others would have have nothing to say to the plan, they marched off to a corner by themselves and made their arrangements in excited whispers; while Gipsy and Elspeth looked at each other, and Elaine went on reading without taking in any sense at all.

When, finally, the rebels had vanished, Gipsy went up to the school-captain.

"Elaine!"

Elaine never raised her head, but she did mumble, "Well — what?''

"You heard what Maureen suggested. What are you going to do about it?''

"What can I do?''

"Report them," said Elspeth.

"I'm not going to tell tales, And besides, it's all talk. Maureen will never dare to do it when it comes to the point. Now go away, and leave me to enjoy my book in peace.''

The pair looked at each other. Then Gipsy tried again. "I don't think you're quite right in saying Maureen won't dare, Elaine. I honestly believe that she and one or two of the others will try it on. Can't we stop them! It'll be so awfully bad for everyone concerned if we don't.''

''Oh, bother you!'' snapped Elaine. ''If you're as keen as all that, stop them yourself! I'm sure, *I* don't care if you like to sneak. Please yourself *what* you do!'' Gipsy moved away followed by Elspeth.

''What are we going to do?'' she asked dejectedly of the Scottish girl.

''It will be no good talking to Maureen just now,'' said Elspeth. ''She's wild because of the Guides — that will be what is wrong with Elaine too — and she's going to take out her disappointment this way.''

''Oh, those Guides!'' groaned Gipsy. ''As if we didn't *all* want them!''

''Do you really think Maureen will give up the idea when it comes to the point, as Elaine says? Or do you think she'll just go on?''

''No saying,'' returned Gipsy dejectedly. ''Maureen's a wild Irisher when her dander's up! She's capable of doing anything!''

Finally, they decided to do nothing, but to watch and, if possible, to stop the girls from leaving the house after tea. And, most unfairly, they blamed all this trouble to the fact that the Chalet School had Guides, while the Saints had none.

CHAPTER ELEVEN

Joey Acts

It was five o'clock in the afternoon — or seventeen by continental time — and Joey Bettany was up in her dormitory with the rest of her clan, changing for the evening. They had had a glorious time on the ice that afternoon. Jo always maintained that the first skating was the best, and she was arguing this out with Frieda Mensch, who refused to see it, when her eyes were suddenly caught by some dark figures on the lake near the old tree that overhung it, not far from St Scholastika's. "I say!" she exclaimed. "See that!"

Frieda, Mary, and Simone crowded to her cubicle to look out of the window, while Marie von Eschenau, who had the other 'lake-window' cubicle, promptly went to hers.

"But there are people skating there!" cried Frieda. "That is where the big spring is, and no one ever goes there, for the ice is never safe! Who *can* they be?"

Jo shook her head, and looked up the lake to the St Scholastika's end, where a warm glow betokened the blazing of a huge bonfire. The same had been lighted at the Seespitz end, and in both parts skaters crowded the ice. It was a clear night and the stars shone frostily in the sky, giving a pale light, which enabled the girls to see as far over the lake as was possible from their windows. The moon was not yet up, but when it rose the ice would be covered with people from all round. But everyone would avoid that part by the tree and the part near the dripping rock, for there lay the two biggest springs which helped to fill the lake. Skating there was never safe, and the people living in the two hamlets always struck out well to the centre before they turned in any direction.

"It must be the Saints," said Mary at last. "But didn't anyone warn them?"

"I'm sure Herr Braun would," replied Joey. "Look how he came to tell my sister that first winter. What *are* we to do?"

"Tell Mademoiselle," suggested Simone. "She will then ring up Miss Browne, who will at once call them in and take them to a safer part."

There was silence, and Mary looked at Joey. Simone caught the glance, and at once her grave little face became graver.

"Do you mean that you think they are there without the knowledge of Miss Browne?" she asked.

"Well, what does it look like?" asked Mary. "It's rather dark — *we* are never allowed to skate except in the daytime, and I don't suppose Miss Browne will think differently from Mademoiselle on *that* point. They're in a most dangerous part, and we can be sure that they have been warned. They've broken out — little asses! And —"

She was interrupted by the banging of the door. Joey had flown, just as she was, in her dressing-gown, her hair standing all dishevelled, and only one stocking on, straight to the study to find Mademoiselle.

The others went back to their own cubicles and went on with their dressing soberly. It was out of their hands now. Or so they thought. They were mistaken, however. Ten minutes later, Jo came tearing back, and, casting aside her dressing-gown, was scrambling into the rest of her clothes. "Wires down!" she panted, as she struggled into a frock — *any* frock! "Mademoiselle and Maynie are off to Le Petit Chalet . . . some of the kids there are out in spots, an' it looks like measles! Bill's gone to Innsbruck for the week-end, and Nally's gone up to the Sonnalpe to see Madge about something or other . . . and there isn't a *soul* to settle those idiots over there but *us*!"

The prefects gasped in horror. Then Mary made for the door.

"But where are you going?" demanded Marie.

"To get my outdoor things! — Jo, you skate better than most of us — you and Frieda! Buck up, and skate across and tell them! I'm going round the lake to St Scholastika's to tell someone to fetch them in."

She was off, and the door banged behind her, just as Simone cried, "But Jo! You promised Madame on your Guide honour that you would never go off again without telling someone in authority!"

Jo stopped, her face white with worry. "So I did!"

"That cannot be helped," declared Frieda with unexpected decision. "Madame would never expect you to wait when there was life in danger."

"I'll have to go!" said Jo. "Madge will understand, I know."

She finished her dressing, and made for the door, followed by Frieda.

Marie ran to the window and looked out. "They are still at it," she announced. "They cannot skate at all, and they are just falling about. The ice will not stand much of *that*!"

"I'm going to Mademoiselle," said Deira shortly. "She ought to know." The next minute she too had gone.

It was a case where action had to be taken swiftly. There could be no doubt that the Saints were in actual danger.

The anxious people in the Green dormitory at the Chalet still thronged round the window, and were presently rewarded by seeing Joey Bettany at the edge of the lake, getting into her skating-boots as quickly as she could. Frieda followed almost at once. The girls in the dormitory clutched at each other as they watched the scene. The Saints were still tumbling about, trying to get their balance. They made nothing of the long flaws that were beginning to form in the ice. It is true that Doris looked at them rather uneasily once or twice, but when she drew Maureen's attention to them, she only shook her off with an exclamation of impatience. Maureen was beginning to find that she could keep up better if she leaned forward a little, and was deeply interested in her own progress.

Joey and Frieda, skating fast, reached the limits of the safe ice, and then paused, and Frieda gave a call. "St Scholastika's! *Hé*, there!"

No one paid any attention, and Joey skated slowly round the boundary, trying to get near. Her years in the Tyrol had taught her what those long shining marks on the black ice meant.

"What are we to do?" cried Frieda in German. Judging from the cracks that were appearing in all directions it would not be long before it gave, and there would be a catastrophe.

Joey recognized Maureen at this moment, and, balancing herself carefully, shouted, "Maureen — Maureen, I say! Get off this ice! It's dangerous!"

Maureen, startled by hearing her own name from a strange person, looked across and went down once more. The ice creaked and groaned as she landed on it, and she suddenly woke up to the danger. Unaccustomed to tackling things in an emergency, she lost her head and began to scream. Joey saw no help for it. Lowering herself till she lay at full length, she began wriggling her way over the bending ice to the group of startled girls. As she did so, she called to them to get to the shore at once. Frieda followed her example; and one or two of the elder Saints who had managed to keep their wits about them began to stagger to the shore, leading such of the middles as they could catch. The others at once followed them, and they were all more or less safe, leaving only Maureen, still lying huddled up and screaming, on the dangerous part, when the ice suddenly seemed to give a tremendous heave; there was a cracking and a groaning, and then a splash and Jo and Maureen were struggling in the water.

The first shock of the icy water nearly robbed Jo of her senses. Maureen, promptly fainted from horror, and the slighter girl bent all her energies to grabbing at her and holding her up, while she tried to tread water. Jo was an excellent swimmer, hours of practice during the summer having made her expert; but she soon found that swimming in summer weather, when the sun is shining down with a glorious glow and one is hampered by nothing heavier than a swimming suit, is a totally different matter from trying to swim in water that is full of broken ice, laden with another girl who is unconscious, and both clad in winter garments all well-soaked through, with skates in addition. Also, swimming by the light of the stars is a difficult matter at any time. Now it made things even more appalling than they already were. Jo began to sink beneath the weight she was bearing, and it seemed to her that the cruel numbing cold was creeping up to her heart and stopping it. She cast one wild agonized look round for Frieda, but could not see her. The girls on shore were mostly screaming with terror, though one or two of them were trying to pull branches off one of the old trees. Meantime, Joey Bettany of the Chalet School was obviously weakening, and Maureen lay — limp, grey, and to all appearance dead — across her shoulder. The freezing cold was doing its work, and Joey knew that she was gradually losing consciousness. It scarcely seemed worth while to struggle as she was doing. It was so vain, and soon it would be all over. Vaguely she wondered what Madge would say when they told her. Dick would be upset too, and the Babies would never remember "Auntie Joey."

It was at this moment she heard a cry and managed to turn round. Frieda had worked her way round to the nearest point of safety, and now lay prone on the ice, her arms held out, her skate-tips digging desperately for a hold. "Joey!" she gasped. "Swim this way! I can hold you up till help comes!"

Joey tried, but she was too numbed with cold to manage, and the whole affair might have ended in tragedy had it not been for a newcomer, who was running swiftly along the road from Seespitz, where he had been summoned to attend to a sick child. They discovered later that he had met Mary, had caught her words, enough to understand the drift of them, and had torn away at full speed to render what help he could, leaving her to go to St Scholastika's with her message.

At the same time help came from the other direction, as two men, carrying a rope, came flying over the ice, and while one lay down and wriggled onwards, the other coiled the rope tightly and hung it so that the noosed end went well over Jo's head and shoulders, and then drew tight with a jerk that made her feel as if she were being sawn in two. With a little gasp she fainted, but by this time the one who was lying prone had caught the line and was drawing the two girls towards the safer ice. Then, still on his face, for the ice groaned so beneath his weight that he dared not change his position, he writhed round till he reached the bank, and there the stranger was waiting to help him. Between them they lifted out the two girls, who were tightly roped together by the noose, and then, while the peasant picked up Maureen, the other man picked up Joey, and, leaving the third to see to Frieda, they staggered off to St Scholastika's with the two girls.

How the peasant ever managed to walk on skates, was marvelled at afterwards when anyone had time to remember it. Somehow, he did it, and the two men passed up the short path and in at the door Miss Browne was holding open, followed by a long string of white-faced weeping girls.

"In here," was all she said, opening the door of her own little sanctum, where a huge fire blazed on the hearth. "This is the best place till Matron has beds ready for them. I have sent word to her. Girls, go and take your things off, and go to the form-rooms."

The two men brought in their burdens, and Mary Burnett, white and horrified, followed into the room, dropped down beside Joey.

The man from Seespitz came and bent over the younger girl. "Joey!" he cried. "But what is she doing here?"

Mary looked up. It was Gottfried Mensch, come down from the Sonnalpe. All the Chalet girls knew him, and all liked him. He had married the first head-girl, Gisela Marani, in the previous June, and they had a pretty home not far from Die Rosen, the Russells' chalet. Gottfried was next best to Dr Jem, as all the girls called Dr Russell, and Mary felt a little more hopeful as he bent over her friend.

Presently, he left her to Mary and Miss Soames who had come in, to undress, and went to Maureen. He examined her, and then stood back. "Get them both to bed as quickly as possible," he said brusquely. "Hot baths first, and get me some *Schnapps* at once, and hot water."

"There is no brandy in the house," said Miss Browne, whitening again. "Matron keeps salvolatile, but we have no spirit at all."

Gottfried turned to his helper of the lake. "Get some," he said.

The man nodded, and made off at top speed. The girls were carried off to the bathroom, where they were put into hot baths, and then rolled in blankets heated at the fires, and hot-water bottles were laid round them. Gottfried came into the sick-room when they were there, and called Mary to follow him. "You are a Guide. See, you must rub Joey over the heart, *so*. Keep on doing it till I tell you to stop."

Mary got on to the bed and began the regular massaging at once. Her own heart was full of dread, but she knew that this was no time for giving way to her own feelings. So she worked steadily on, while Matron did the same to Maureen.

A little later, the man came back with the spirits for which the young doctor had sent, and he wet the lips, temples, and nostrils of the two girls. Meantime, Miss Soames and Miss Elliott had come forward and volunteered their services, explaining that they, too, were Guides. Gottfried accepted them, and the work went on. A message had been sent to the Chalet

School to Mademoiselle Lepâttre, and she came at once. Frieda, who had been brought to St Scholastika's by the second peasant, was in the senior common-room with Gipsy, very quiet, very tense.

It seemed a life-time, almost, to those who were waiting, before the young doctor ceased from his labours and said, in a low voice, "Thank God! They are living!"

When it became evident that life was flickering up stronger in both, he left them to the care of their nurses for just long enough to see and reassure Mademoiselle, and to send the men up to Die Rosen with a message for Mrs Russell, who, he knew, would want to come to her sister as soon as possible. Miss Browne, looking ten years older, came down, and sent the girls off to bed. Miss Anderson volunteered to take Mary and Frieda back to the Chalet School, and also to bear any messages Mademoiselle might wish to send. Mademoiselle was glad to avail herself of this kind offer, and so a cautious message was sent to Miss Maynard, and the trio set off.

All that night Gottfried stayed where he was, in the sick-room, and by morning he had a report ready. Maureen was already in the throes of a sharp attack of rheumatic-fever, and Joey Bettany was down with pleuro-pneumonia.

CHAPTER TWELVE

A Terrible Week

From that day onwards till the end of October, it seemed to the girls of both schools as if they lived, ate, and slept in an atmosphere of black anxiety. All differences were forgotten when they met, for the one thing they could think of was the sick-room at St Scholastika's and its two occupants.

Madge Russell came down the day after the accident, accompanied by her husband. Miss Maynard's brother was left in charge at the Sonnalpe for the day, and either Dr Russell or Dr Mensch would return that evening. At Mademoiselle's suggestion the St Scholastika girls were drafted off to the Chalet School, with three of the staff to help the Chalet School staff, and the house was given over to the patients. Mercifully, it had been discovered that the spots on the Chalet School juniors were nothing worse than a bilious rash, so there was no need to dread measles for them. The ten eldest Saints were left at the school, for they could go on with their work by themselves, and Mademoiselle Berné and Miss Anderson were remaining too. Miss Soames would come out every afternoon to give them maths, and Miss Elliott would come twice a week for music. But all the middles and juniors were packed off as quickly as possible, with Miss Phipps, the junior-mistress, in charge, and the Chalet School found itself unexpectedly crowded. Ordinarily this would have been the signal for all sorts of amazing pranks on the part of the younger ones. But now no one had time to think of anything but Joey and Maureen, who were fighting for their lives in the smaller building across the lake. Maureen suffered the most, but it was for Jo that the worst fears were entertained. Her long-continued delicacy was against her, and then her highly-strung temperament kept her fever running at a height which, the doctors were agreed, could not continue for long, for the heart would not stand the strain.

Twice daily eight girls walked round the lake for news, and every time they came back looking gloomier than they had left. Maureen's father — she was a motherless girl — had been cabled for, and Mrs Russell was with Jo night and day. Dr Jem had sent for good old Dr Erckhardt, who had pulled Joey through two illnesses during the early days of the Chalet School and who understood her. He came at once, and Dr Russell went back to the Sonnalpe, where he had some bad cases, which he dared not leave for long. Dr Erckhardt would not commit himself either way, but, to Madge's frightened eyes, he looked very grave over the condition of both girls.

They had moved Maureen to a room far away from Joey, for her cries of pain disturbed the other girl, even when she was unconscious herself, and they dared risk nothing. The Irish child was very ill, but Jo's danger was more immediate.

"If only God lets Jo get well, I will never be naughty again," said the Robin to Miss Durrant on the Monday night, when she was being put to bed.

"You must pray very hard to our Lady and the blessed Saints that they will intercede for her with our Lord," replied Miss Durrant, who was a devout Catholic.

"Oh, I *will*!" said the Robin earnestly. "I did at prayers this morning, and I have said the Rosary for her five times today already. If I pray hard enough, don't you think God will let us keep her?"

"We will hope so, *mein Blümchen*," said the mistress tenderly. "Now you must lie down and go to sleep."

The elder girls were not quite so outspoken, but they, too, prayed long and earnestly that day, and many other days, that Joey might be spared to them. Simone went about with a face so swollen with crying that she could scarcely see, and Frieda became quieter than ever, and went off into corners to be by herself.

As for the Saints, they, too, thought much and deeply during those anxious days when it seemed as if Maureen and Jo would not come back to them. Some of the elder ones looked after Maureen's little sister, and did their best to comfort her.

Then came the fifth day when, as they all knew, the crisis was at hand with Jo. Dr Jem had come down from the Sonnalpe early in the morning, and would stay at Buchau till the next day. Gottfried Mensch, who had been at Buchau the previous day, skated across the lake to the Chalet to see his little sister and tell her the latest news. Jo was very ill — it was as grave as it could possibly be; but she had seemed just a tiny shade stronger the last three hours. It was all the comfort he had to give the Chalet people, and it was cold comfort. Maureen was very ill, too, but her fever was down a point, and she had always been a sturdy healthy girl, with plenty of vitality on which to fall back. She suffered badly, but so far, her heart was standing the strain better than they had expected. If she went on as she was doing, they had hopes of her.

"And Joey?" asked Frieda breathlessly. "What of Joey?"

"She is very ill, little sister," said Gottfried gently. "We must all pray the dear God that she may live."

Frieda turned away from him. She knew now that they had very little hope that Jo's strength would hold out, and Jo was as dear to her as her own sister Bernhilda, who was in far-away Vienna.

Gottfried left the Chalet and went off up the mountain slopes to the Sonnalpe, to be greeted by all those who knew Jo with eager questions about her. His report to Jack Maynard was more explicit. "I do not think there is any chance. The fever has never ceased to run high the whole time, and the heart cannot stand the strain. She is a shade stronger these last few hours, but I fear lest it be only a partial rally before the end."

At St Scholastika's all pretence at work had been given up. The girls had been told how ill Joey was only that morning,

103

and it was filling their thoughts to the exclusion of everything else. Miss Anderson said, "We will walk round to the Chalet School with the latest news. Be sure you wrap up well — there is a bitter wind."

They did as they were told in listless silence. The mistress saw them out of the room, and then went to get on her own things and to inquire what the last bulletin from the sick-room was. She met Miss Browne on the stairs and explained what she had done. "The girls cannot work," she said. "I honestly think they will be better outside for a time. Will you find out what the doctors think of Joey and Maureen now, and then we will go round to the Chalet School with the news. It will give us an object for our walk at least."

"I have just seen Dr Erckhardt," replied Miss Browne sadly. "He says that she is as ill as she can possibly be. Maureen is a shade easier, and has been sleeping for an hour. We must be thankful for so much; but if Joey Bettany dies, I shall feel that I am largely to blame, for the girls ought never to have been left to themselves as they have been. Had they been properly supervised they could not have gone out as they did, and then this would never have happened."

Miss Anderson looked thoughtful. "I don't think that is altogether your fault," she said. "I understand that the Chalet girls have quite as much freedom as our girls. If you will forgive my saying so, Miss Browne, I think part of the trouble lies in the fact that our girls wanted more than we have given them."

"But what more could we give them than they have had?" asked Miss Browne. "They have a good library, games, a debating society. What more can they want?"

Miss Anderson said, "I do think they need something more than they have — the something more that Guides would give them. I am not a Guide myself, but I know what tremendous good they have done wherever they have been started. Miss

104

Browne, won't you think about starting them here — in this school — once this dreadful time is over?"

"I may begin them," said Miss Browne. "But I am afraid it will be — too late."

Miss Anderson shook her head. "You must not say that," she said firmly. "While there is life, there is always hope. I have been talking to Mrs Russell, and she tells me that Joey has pulled through serious illnesses before this. Let us pray that she may pull through this one."

She turned then, and went on up the stairs, leaving her Head a little comforted by her words. The sound of feet crunching over the crisp snow drew her attention as she put on her cap, and, looking out of the window, she saw Dick Bettany, whom they had sent for the previous night. His fair boyish face looked suddenly old, and there was little spring in his step as he moved. She had never met him before, but she knew who he must be, for though Madge was dark of hair and eyes, and her twin was fair, there was a strong resemblance between them. Miss Anderson picked up her gloves and ran downstairs to let him in. His brown eyes questioned hers imploringly as she opened the door for him. "She is very ill," she said at once, "but all hope is not lost. Come in, Mr Bettany, and I will send someone to you."

Miss Anderson ran upstairs and was fortunate enough to find Dr Jem coming out of the sick-room. "Mr Bettany is here," she said.

Jem turned sharply. "Dick here?" he said in carefully lowered tones. "Thank Heaven for that! Madge will be needing him before long, I am afraid."

Miss Anderson's fresh colour faded. "Is — is it so bad?" she faltered.

"It is as bad as it can possibly be," he said gravely. "She is raving now, and — the heart will not stand the strain."

With a sick feeling the mistress stood aside to let him go

downstairs, and then went down to the girls. She dared not tell them what he had said, but her face spoke for her.

Gipsy suddenly burst into tears. "Oh, Miss Anderson!" she cried. "Is there *no* hope at all?"

"She is very ill," said Miss Anderson. "Try not to cry, Gipsy. You cannot help matters at all that way."

Gipsy choked back her tears and dried her eyes. They took partners and went out. Just as they had turned the corners by the water-meadows, they saw a small girl come running along. Her brown coat was fastened up over a red scarf, and her brown beret was crushed down over thick black curls, while her lovely little face was flushed with cold and exercise. Everyone recognized Robin Humphries at once, and Miss Anderson caught her.

"Robin!" she cried. "Where are you going?"

The Robin wriggled free at once and stood a little distance off. "To Joey!" she said.

At once, before anyone could stop her, she was off again running at the full speed of her short legs, and Miss Anderson stopped any pursuit. "Dr Russell and Mr Bettany are both there," she said. "Leave her to them. Meantime, I think we had better hurry to the Chalet. I don't suppose she had permission to come, and they may be worrying about her."

Meanwhile, in the senior common-room at St Scholastika's, Dr Jem was breaking to Dick Bettany the news of his little sister's serious condition. "She is as ill as she can be," he said. "She is so ill that, candidly, Dick, I doubt if she will see the afternoon."

Dick groaned. "Oh, Jem, old chap! It hits hard!"

Jem took a turn or two across the room before he answered. "Very hard," he said at last, clearing his throat. "Do you think I don't know that? One gets pretty fond of Joey in no time. And Madge—"

He stopped, unable to go on, and there was no need for further words. Dick knew as well as Jem did just what Joey was to her sister. He sat staring into the fire, misery in his face. Jem stood gazing out of the window, seeing nothing at all. He never noticed a small figure in the Chalet brown come running up the path, and the two were considerably startled when the door of the room opened and a curly-headed person appeared, very much out of breath with all her haste and ran across the room to Jem.

"Oncle Jem! I want to see Joey!"

Jem stooped and picked her up. "Robin! How did you get here?"

"I ran," said the Robin, putting an arm round his neck. "Oncle Jem, let me see Joey. Me, I will sing her Mamma's song, and then she will go to sleep fast — fast!"

Jem shook his head. "Joey is too ill to see you darling. She wouldn't know you if you went in."

"But let me *try*," pleaded the Robin. "Oh, Oncle Jem, *let* me try!"

Jem set her down. Dick looked up suddenly. "Oh, let the kid try, Jem," he said. "If Joey is as ill as that, it can't make much difference."

Jem nodded. "There is just the chance that Robin's voice may rouse her. They are very fond of each other. Take your things off, Robin, and warm yourself."

Robin wriggled out of her cap and coat, held her hands out for two minutes to the blaze, and then marched over to the door. "Me, I am ready," she announced.

Jem followed her, his arm through Dick's, and so the three reached the door of the sick-room, and went in.

Everything was very spotless. By the bed sat Madge, all the colour drained out of her cheeks, her dark eyes full of agony, as she sat there, one slim hand holding Joey's. Robin's eyes wandered past to the bed and its occupant. Joey lay propped up with pillows to relieve the breathing. Her black eyes were half-open, and her cheeks were scarlet. A tearing rusty sound came through her parted lips, and she was muttering to herself in low tones.

The Robin ran forward and climbed up on to the bed. She possessed herself of the other hot hand, and leaned over. "Joey, I am going to sing you to sleep with Mamma's song. You must close your eyes and go to sleep."

The black eyes opened a little wider, and the grown-up people in the room held their breath. Could it be possible that the Robin's baby voice was going to break the delirium where all else had failed? It looked like it. There was something in the black eyes that had not been there for five long days.

The Robin bent forward again, and laid her chubby hand over them. "You must shut your eyes, Joey, or you won't go to sleep. Now do as I tell you, *d'reckly*!"

She took her hand away, and the long-lashed lids were shut, the black lashes making a startling half-circle on the crimson cheeks. But Madge now kneeling by the side of the bed, praying with all her heart that this might succeed where all else had failed, felt the tenseness of the hot hand relaxing a little.

Satisfied with Joey's obedience, the Robin lifted up her baby voice in the old Russian folk-song. 'The Red Sarafan.' Joey lay still at last, her eyes close shut. No one dared to move or speak as the Robin sang on, and, meantime the harsh sounds were surely softening a little, the crimson flush on the hollow cheeks was a little paler.

Struck by a sudden awful thought Jem moved forward at last and laid his hand quietly on the slim wrist. It was cooler and it didn't seem quite so dry. His finger moved to the pulse. For a moment he could hardly feel it. Then a sudden throb of joy leapt in his heart, for it was stronger than it had been an hour ago, and also quieter.

"Go on singing Robin," said Jem softly. "Don't stop till I tell you."

The Robin went on. She sang the song through five times.

Then Jem laid his finger on her lips to hush her, and she became perfectly still. A hush fell on the room, where even the sound of Joey's breathing seemed to have died away.

For one awful moment Madge thought that it was the end. Then her eyes went to the quiet face. The dark flush had faded — Joey was lying easily and comfortably, her lips slightly parted, one hand pillowing her cheek. She looked very peaceful as she lay there, and the tears that the elder sister felt should have fallen would not come. Then her husband was bending over her, and drawing her away from the bedside, while Dick, the Robin in his arms, was following them. When they had passed from the room to Matron's which opened out of it, Jem closed the door. His wife looked at him mutely. "All's well dearest," he said. "Joey is sleeping, her pulse is stronger and the fever is broken. I believe we shall save her." Then he caught her — just in time for the shock was too much for Madge Russell in her worn-out state, and she had fainted.

When she came to herself again, she was lying on Matron's bed and Dick was with her. He was mopping his eyes with a handkerchief of flaring orange and his lips were quivering as he turned to her. "All serene old lady! Jem's just gone back to her, and he'll be in again in a minute."

"Was it the crisis?" asked Madge faintly. But Dick didn't know.

She got up and pushed the hair back off her face. "I must go to her, Dick. Don't try to stop me."

However someone else came just then who was able to stop her most effectually. Jem had summoned Dr Erckhardt to the sickroom, and he had pronounced that the danger was past. The fever was broken; the inflammation subsiding; and, ere long, Joey would be completely out of danger.

CHAPTER THIRTEEN

Celebrations

"For goodness' sake, Cornelia, get *out* of the way! That was very nearly your fingers!"

"Well, I want to help. Give me something to do, Mary."

"Mary — *Mary*! I've been yelling at you for ten minutes — very nearly! Do listen!"

Mary Burnett turned round from the spray of evergreen she was fastening over a window in the Green dormitory, and cast an exasperated glance at Marie von Eschenau, who had come running into the room. At Mary's side stood Cornelia Flower, a bunch of many-coloured ribbons in her hand and a most unbecoming frown on her face. At the other "lake" window was Frieda Mensch, with Simone Lecoutier, trimming the frame with ivy. Over Joey's bed was a huge card with 'Welcome back' painted on it in scarlet letters outlined in gold, and the bedposts were wreathed round with more ivy.

The secret of all this was that Jo was coming back to the Chalet after an absence of six weeks, and the girls were busy decorating for her. They had been at it all the morning, which, luckily, was a Saturday, and she was expected in an hour's time, and the dormitory was still not ready.

Once she had turned the corner, Jo had got well with the speed with which she always recovered from any illness. A week after that dreadful day on which they had thought they were going to lose her, she was demanding to be propped up in bed, and a fortnight after that she was making a fuss because they wouldn't let her get up. Once she *did* reach the getting-up stage she progressed by leaps and bounds, till the last week of November saw her being carried up to the Sonnalpe for a week's holiday before she came back to school. Madge had wanted to keep her for the rest of the term, but Joey had no mind to lose any of the fun. Accordingly, as there was only three weeks left, Mrs Russell had decided to bring her small son and come to the Chalet herself. She would take her old classes, and resume, for the time being, her old Headship, much to the joy of everyone. Above all, she would keep an eye on her young sister and see that she did not over-exert herself. Mademoiselle was thankful to hear this, as she was quite worn out with all that had happened that term. If Mrs Russell were at the helm the responsibility would be off her shoulders, and she felt that she could take a rest. Hence, therefore, all the excitement and confusion in the Chalet School, and Mary's worried look.

Marie von Eschenau, as pretty as ever, and not a great deal taller than the day on which she had first come to the Chalet School, three years ago, came forward now, holding out a letter, at sight of which Mary dropped her hammer and tacks and sprang forward with a cry of joy. "From Grizel! Oh, thank you, Marie!"

Frieda and Simone left their work at once, and raced up to her. "From Grizel, Mary? Oh, do open it and see what she has to say," implored Frieda, her pretty face all smiles.

Mary ripped open the envelope and slipped out the letter. Grizel was by no means a good correspondent, and this epistle was no exception to the general rule of her letters. Mary read aloud:

Dear Everyone, — I was thankful to get your last letters telling me that Jo is so much better, and is coming back to school so soon. It wouldn't be her if she didn't do something daft! I hope she's satisfied this time!

Now for my news. My lessons finish this week, and I'm not going to England for Christmas, as my people are going to be away. So I've written to Madame, to ask if I may come to the Chalet for the rest of term, and then I'm going off to Gisela for a week, to Bernhilda for a week, and to Wanda for a week. I shall be sick of train-journeys by the time it's all over, I suppose, but it'll be worth it to see you all again.

The people here are awfully jolly, and I've made one friend — an English girl named Geraldine Challoner, only she generally answers to 'Gerry.' She's a positive marvel, and Signor d'Affizzio can't say enough about her. I may bring her with me. She's dying to see the Tyrol and can't go home, as all the younger ones are indulging in scarlet-fever, so they won't have her. She is going to stay at the Albrecht for the rest of term, but for the hols she is going to Innsbruck, to stay with another pal of ours here — a girl named Meuda Melnarti, who is a sister of Klara.

Expect me when you see me, and be prepared to welcome Gerry, whom I know you'll like.

Best love to everyone, especially Joey and the Robin, from   GRIZEL.

"Grizel coming back!" cried Marie. "Oh, how nice that will be!" And I, too, am to go to Wanda for a week, so I shall ask that it may be the week she goes there!"

"A new girl?" said Mary thoughtfully. "I wonder what she'll be like?"

Then, moved to a sudden realization of how time was going, all dashed back to their work.

They were still in the thick of it when a voice was heard calling up the stairs for them, and the five prefects, forgetting their dignity, all made a rush and grabbed Joey at the foot of the stairs. A thin Joey she was, and she had grown during her illness, so that she was nearly an inch and a half taller than she had been. She was still very pale, but her eyes were gleaming in the old way, and she answered their questions and greetings with all the old slang, despite the fact that Madame had, from the very first, forbidden most slang.

112

"Hello, everyone! Topping to see you all again! Have we got our school to ourselves again, or do we still share with the baby Saints?"

"No; they went back last week," said Mary. "Maureen is much better, and they have taken her away by slow stages to the Riviera for a year. After that, the doctor thinks she will be all right. Have you heard about Grizel? Isn't it topping?"

"Heard *what* about Grizel?" demanded Joey, stopping at the top of the stairs. "Madge has had a letter from her this morning, but she's never said anything about it to me. What's she been doing?"

"She's coming here for the rest of the term," explained Mary. "She said she'd written to Madame to ask her. And she's bringing a chum with her — an English girl she calls Gerry Challoner, who's a good pianist."

Joey sat down on her bed, and gazed round her appreciatively. "I say! You've made this place look marvellous! Thanks awfully!"

Simone came and sat down beside her. "I am so glad to have you again, *ma mie*! You must not go on the ice again, Joey, no matter if *fifty* girls are drowning!"

"I'm going skating just as soon as they allow me!" replied Joey cheerfully. "However, that won't be this term, so you needn't worry, Simone. Let's change the subject — it isn't a pleasant one. How's the play going?"

"Not too badly," said Mary, leaning on the bed-rail. "Of course, all the parts have had to be moved round a bit, thanks to you, but it's all right now."

"Who's got my part?" asked Joey.

"Cornelia. She has a lovely voice, though it's not so good as yours, and Plato decided on her. She's very impressed, and awfully pleased with herself."

"She would be! It's a nuisance that I can't do it, but I get tired still, and it wouldn't be fair to the play. I might let it down." Joey got up, and began to brush her straight black hair firmly.

"What a length you are growing, Jo!" said Mary.

"I can see over my sister's head," returned Jo. "Well, I'm off now to see Deira and the others. I wonder when Griselda will turn up. It'll be fun seeing her again, won't it?"

"We are all looking forward to it — when we have had time to forget that we are just welcoming you," said Frieda quaintly. "But tell me, Jo, how are Gottfried and Gisela?"

"Very fit. They sent their love to you, and you are to go up, when we break up, and spend a few days with them before you go to Innsbruck," said Jo.

"I shall be very glad," said the Austrian girl seriously. "It is lonely at home — now that Bernhilda has gone away to Wien."

Jo nodded, and went out of the room to seek Deira in the Blue dormitory, and to be welcomed back. From there she went on to the Green Dormitory, where she had slept for so many terms, and was straightway embroiled in an argument with Margia about Herr Anserl, with whom that young lady had had a battle royal the day before. Margia declared he was an old bear; Jo insisted that he was dear, and that Margia simply *asked* for all the trouble she got. Madge Russell, coming in search of her sister, heard them hard it it, and sat down on the stairs to laugh at the sounds that proceeded from the room. Then, remembering that Jem had warned her not to let Jo overtire herself, she got up, and went in.

"You're a pig-headed little ass!" Jo was proclaiming. "I only wonder the old lamb doesn't wring your neck for you some time or other! I jolly well should!"

"Jo!" said Madge in an awful voice. "What is the rule about slang?"

Jo spun round on her heel, and looked decidedly crestfallen. "I — I forgot," she said lamely.

Madge looked at her. "Forgetfulness is a very poor excuse," she said. "In a prefect it is shameful! In any case, neither of you ought to be here now. The bell is just going to ring for *Kaffee*. Run downstairs, both of you, and kindly don't let me hear such language from either of you again."

With Madge in that mood, Jo dared not argue, so she went off, feeling that she had indeed stepped down from her position as interesting invalid to that of a mere schoolgirl. Margia only waited to pat her hair with her brush, and then she followed meekly.

Madge followed after, a smile on her lips. The weeks that had passed had restored her colour and the slender roundness that she had lost during the terrible five days when she had feared that Joey was going to leave her. Now that fear was over, and Jo seemed well on the way to being stronger than she had ever been before.

The bell rang for *Kaffee* as she reached the foot of the stairs, and she went off to the study, where the staff were waiting for her, while from the *Speisesaal* came the sound of girlish voices that she had always loved. Luise had made special cakes to celebrate the return of Fräulein Joey and Madame, and there was *Blaubeeren* jam too.

Kaffee was over by the time the girls were ready to go and change for the evening dancing, but the mistresses were not inclined to hurry. Suddenly there came the sound of light feet along the passage, and then giggles outside the door, followed by a tap.

Madge sat up in the chair in which she had been lounging, and the staff followed her example. "Come in!" she called.

The door opened and Joey, followed by the Robin, tumbled into the room. Rufus, the great St Bernard, Joey's best-loved possession, trotted in after them and sat down beside the big stove, smiling amiably on the assembled company. Usually he lived up on the Sonnalpe, but he had accompanied his young mistress to school for what remained of the term, to his joy as well as hers.

"Well, Jo, what is it?" asked Madge.

"If you please, Madame," began Joey, very properly, "the Robin and I are a deputation."

The woman held out her hand to the Robin. "Are you really? Come here, Robin."

The Robin ran forward. "Please, Madame, we want to show the — I mean, St Scholastika's, that we are sorry we were rude to them in the beginning, and may we do something?" she asked.

"What do you want to do?" asked Madge, with a smile of amusement.

"Have a party or something," said Jo, standing bolt upright, with her hands behind her.

"You must ask Mademoiselle that."

"Well, may we please, Mademoiselle?"

"But, my child, I must consider," protested Mademoiselle. "And I do not know that Miss Browne would permit her girls to come."

"She might," said the Robin. "She was quite nice to me when I saw her last Sunday. And we've been living together, and they are not so bad!"

"I will consider," repeated Mademoiselle. "And now you must go and change your dresses, or you will be late for supper."

Joey opened her mouth to protest, but she caught her sister's eye, and subsided. She and the Robin left the room, followed by Rufus, and closed the door behind them.

"How like old times!" sighed the ex-Head. "Isn't Jo a length?"

"Tremendous!" laughed Miss Wilson. "As for old times, Madame, we all wish they might come back, if they would bring you back to us."

"That is impossible!" laughed her Head. "Well, I must go and bath my son and put him to bed. He's been very good with

116

Rosa all this time, hasn't he? But I did want to see you all, and Master David is an engrossing young person when he's in the room.''

Miss Durrant and Mademoiselle Lachenais went off first, for they had to go over to Le Petit Chalet to help Matron there to superintend the toilets of the juniors. Miss Wilson, Miss Stewart, and Miss Nalder followed them, and finally there were left only the three who had begun the Chalet School among them.

"We have done well," said Mademoiselle.

No one asked what her meaning was, for they all knew.

"I wonder if St Scholastika's will do as well," said Miss Maynard.

Madge turned to her. "What do you mean, Mollie?"

"What I say. I don't think they will ever be serious rivals to us, you know; but I'm beginning to wonder if they will even last. Maureen has gone, and that small sister of hers; and two or three others are not coming back to them either. I met Miss Soames yesterday, and she tells me that Miss Browne is beginning to doubt her wisdom in coming here. I'll tell you what it is," she went on. "I don't mind betting you what you like, Madge, that they finish at the end of the year!"

"I hope not!" said Madge. "Hasn't Miss Browne put all her money into that place?"

Miss Maynard shook her head. "That I can't tell you. But the accident has frightened some of the parents, Miss Soames thinks, and − well, they aren't a large school as it is; and, of course, we stand in their way. I wonder how things will go."

"There's David," said his mother, who had not heard the last sentence, for she had been listening to her son's voice upraised in a determined outcry for her.

Miss Maynard laughed. "Oh, David has the best part of your heart now, there's no denying. Go to him, my dear. − Mademoiselle, you and I will be *de trop* at this *tête-à-tête*! We'd better go and dress, I think.''

Mademoiselle nodded, and they went out just as Rosa came in carrying her charge. He was a big bonny boy, very like his mother with her dark curls and big dark eyes. He was not at all inclined for bed, but Madge brought to his training the same firmness that had stood her in such good stead with the school, and he was safely in his cot by his usual hour. She changed into a pretty green frock that made her look as much of a girl as little Miss Nalder, who was only twenty-three.

The evening passed as their Saturdays usually did, in dancing, and Jo was indignant because she was made to sit out two-thirds of the time. At nine o'clock dancing was finished, and they stood for prayers.

Just before they began, Mary went up to Mrs Russell. ''If you please, Madame,'' she said shyly, ''we should like you to read a thanksgiving-prayer, if you will, for Jo's return to us.''

Madge nodded, and her eyes shone brightly. ''I will ask Mademoiselle to do so with her girls,'' she said. For Mademoiselle read prayers for the Catholics, and one of the English mistresses always took prayers for the rest.

So prayers were read with the thanksgiving, and when they were over the girls went up to bed, with the old *Gute Nacht* with which they had always been dismissed in the old days. Talking was forbidden on the stairs, so no one was able to voice her feelings at all till they were in the dormitory. Then the prefects gathered in the Green dormitory for a minute.

''It's been a gorgeous coming back,'' said Jo. ''Thanks ever so, all of you.''

CHAPTER FOURTEEN

Informal Celebrations

After that the prefects separated, for they were not supposed to be in each other's rooms at that hour. Deira, Vanna, and Carla went off to their own dormitories, and the other five retired to their cubicles and drew the curtains.

Jo's first care was to strip her bedposts of the decorations. Ivy and evergreens might look very pretty, but for a person who was given to throwing her arms about in her sleep they were not desirable. "I'd have several fits if I grabbed a string of ivy when I was asleep," she explained to the others, as she untwisted the wreaths. "When you wake up suddenly like that, you never are more than half-awake at first, and I'd rather be excused any sensations."

"Perhaps it's as well," agreed Mary, who was getting out of her frock. "I know you, Jo! You'd yell the house down if you did anything of that kind. I, for one, don't want to be awakened by hearing the blood-curdling shrieks you'd be safe to let out!"

"Nor I," added quiet Frieda.

Jo finished her work and piled the greenery in a heap under the bed. She had just finished when a plaintive voice came from the next cubicle. "But has anyone seen my brushes?" it asked.

"*I* haven't," said Marie von Eschenau from the opposite corner. "But what *I* would like to know is where my soap is."

Mary added, "*Who* has been fooling with my comb?"

"Can't you find it?" demanded Joey, drawing aside her curtain and peeping out.

"No; it isn't here, and I know I left it on my bureau when I went down before supper."

"Probably slipped down somewhere," was the suggestion.

Mary hunted, but the comb was not forthcoming, and, by this time, everyone else was lamenting the loss of something necessary. Jo's tooth-brush had gone; Frieda missed her towels; Sophie Hamel, who slept across the landing in a little room with Bianca di Ferrara, came over to inquire if anyone had seen anything of her pyjamas.

"No," said Joey in answer to this last request. "But I'd like to know who has been sewing up my pyjama-case. Just look at it!"

She stalked forth, waving it in the air, and the seniors crowded round to discover that it had been neatly seamed up with the pyjamas inside. At once everyone dashed to look at hers, and the net result was that the seven seniors who occupied the top landing discovered that their cases or their suits had been tampered with. Mary, Marie, Sophie, and Frieda all reported that the legs, sleeves, and necks of their pyjamas had been stitched together; while the others either could not find theirs at all, or else they had been sewn into the cases. They had just made this discovery when Deira came upstairs at a great rate, demanding furiously if anyone had been playing a joke on her, for her sheets had been sewn to the bed, and, what was more, sewn all round.

"Shut up, idiot!" said Joey impolitely. "You'll have the staff here in a minute if you scream like that! Don't you see, you people? It's those little brutes of middles! They *have* done it thoroughly, haven't they?" she went on reflectively. "Go back, Deira, and find out what Carla and Vanna have to report."

Much disgusted, Deira retired, and presently came back with the other two. Carla had lost her dressing-gown. Vanna said sadly that her nightdress had been sewn up everywhere, and she was busy unpicking it when Deira had come into them.

"The *imps*!" said Mary feelingly. "Well, what can we do?"

"Pay them back, of course," returned Joey briskly. "Look here, come in and shut the door. We don't want to drag the staff into this if we can help it. Now then, all of you, *think* like everything, and when you've got an idea, whisper it — don't yell for all the world to hear! We simply must pay them back, I'm hanged if I'll stand this sort of thing!''

They all sat down where they could, and thought deeply. Frieda was the first to make any suggestion. ''Shall we fasten them up in their cubicles, as other people did to us?'' she asked, with a grin at Mary, who had had a hand in that affair.

Jo shook her head. ''Not original! Let's try to get something fresh if we possibly *can*, or they'll think we're lacking in brains!''

''I have thought,'' said Simone slowly, ''but I am sure we ought not to do it, since most of us are prefects.''

''Oh, fiddle!'' retorted Jo, who seemed to have come back with a double portion of impishness since her illness.

''For this one night, I'm going to forget I'm a prefect — at any rate, till we've settled with those middles.''

''Well, do you know where Luise keeps the — the — the flour of corn?''

''D'you mean cornflour by any chance?'' demanded Jo. '''Cos if so, what on earth can we do with cornflour?''

''Powder their hair,'' said Simone. ''Then in the morning, they will awake and wonder what it is that has changed, since they are white-haired in a single night.''

This brilliant idea was greeted with subdued howls of joy. It appealed to them tremendously, and the only drawback was that no one was very sure where the cornflour might be. ''In the storeroom, I should think,'' said Mary, when they had succeeded in overcoming her head-girl's scruples as to the impropriety of such an act.

Their faces fell. The key of the storeroom was kept by Mademoiselle, who gave out stores as they were needed each day. Mademoiselle was known to be a sound sleeper, but even in their present mood no one quite liked to go into her room and abstract her keys.

"There may be some in the cupboard in the *Küche*, suggested Frieda at last. "Shall I go down and see?"

"No; I'll go," said Jo. "Then if anyone arrives, I can think up some excuse quickly."

"You mustn't go, Jo," cried Deira. "You'd get into all sorts of draughts, and catch cold! I'd go meself, but I'd be sure to trip over something — and then they would find out."

"No; I will go," said Frieda determinedly. "If I meet anyone I will say I wanted a drink of water."

With an electric torch in her hand, she set off on her perilous journey, leaving the others all half-suffocated with their laughter at the thought of what the middles would say next morning when they woke up and found that they had turned grey in a single night. Only Mary, of all the crew, had any scruples, and they managed to lull her conscience to sleep for the time being.

Frieda went and returned in safety, and also reported that the staff were having a party of their own in the Head's study, judging by the laughter and chatter she had heard as she came past their door.

"But I found only a little cornflour," she finished, showing the half-filled jar that she had abstracted.

"Never mind; it'll do five or so of them," said Joey, with a wicked grin, as she took it. "Anyway, some of those babies sleep so lightly, that we might have awakened them, and then it would be all up with our little plan. It's a mercy Luise always goes to bed early, isn't it?" she continued. "Now, that will be Cornelia — I *know* she had a hand in it — and Evvy, and — let's see — Yvette, and Anita arranged for. What about the others?"

"Who else would be in it?" asked Carla von Flugen.

"Oh, Signa, Ilonka, Margia, and Suzanne. They are all in the same dormy, and they always hang together. Cyrilla Mazirús and Liebchen von Bruling *might* have helped — I'm not sure. That trio that sleep in the Pink dormy wouldn't have anything to do with it — they're too good! What about the Violets?''

"Hilda Bhaer — too shy," said Deira. "Lieschen Hoffmann and Giovanna Donati? — I don't know. Giovanna might, but she couldn't get away without the others noticing. No, on the whole, I think you may stick to the Yellows and the Blues. Those children are imps!''

"Righto! Then that means we've got to hunt up something that will settle Margia and Suzanne without waking them. The rest won't be so bad.''

"What are we doing to them?'' asked Mary.

"'Fraid we'll have to fall back on Frieda's idea, and stitch those two up into their cubies. As for the others —''

But at this point Mary's conscience suddenly reasserted itself, and she jumped up. "I won't have it!'' she cried. "I think you've all gone mad! Frieda, put that stuff away, and the rest of you go to your own cubies!''

Startled by her sudden vehemence, they handed over the cornflour and did as they were told, but, before they were in bed, one or two of them had time to think. When Mary, after an inquiry as to whether they were all ready, had switched off the light and cuddled down between her own sheets, Joey, Simone, Frieda, and Marie had all made up their minds that they were not going to be frustrated like this in their plans.

Mary, since she was tired, soon dropped off, and slept heavily. At half-past ten the footsteps of the mistresses going to their own rooms could be heard, and when Jo had allowed sufficient time for her sister to have gone safely to bed and to sleep, she slipped out again, and stole into Frieda's cubicle, just as she switched on her torch to go and get the cornflour from Mary's cubicle.

Mercifully for them both, Frieda had plenty of self-control, and the unexpected sight of Jo coming in to her drew no more from her than a smothered exclamation.

"Come on!'' said Jo in a whisper. "I'm not going to be done

like this! We'll get that cornflour and do those kids, and we'll think up something else while we are at it! May as well be hanged for a sheep as a lamb!''

A whisper of ''Joey! Is that you?'' nearly startled them both into betraying themselves, but they bit back their words in time, and then turned to see Simone, followed by Marie, just behind them.

There is no excuse for them, of course. They were among the youngest seniors, it is true, but they were sub-prefects, and they all four knew quite well that what they were about was *not* the thing for prefects, whether full or sub. All that can be said for them is that they were excited by Jo's return, and the pranks of the juniors had added to their excitement. But even so, they should have known better.

However, they were too excited to worry much about it, and in a state of highly suppressed giggles they went out on to the landing, while Mary, her conscience at rest once more, slept the sleep of the just and weary.

On the landing Joey hastily outlined for her friends the scheme she had concocted while waiting for the house to grow quiet. ''We'll do the Green's,'' she said. ''Then, if there's time, we'll do what we can for Ilonka and Cyrilla. Frieda, you move most quietly. You can powder Cornelia and Evadne. Simone, you do Yvette and Anita. Give her half the stuff, Frieda, and for any sake, mind you don't wake them up! Keep it off their faces, and *don't* let it go anywhere near their eyes. We don't want to hurt them — only give them a shock.''

''And the others?'' asked Marie.

''We-ell,'' said the wicked Joey, ''Margia and Suzanne sleep next door — luckily. You know how they both toss about. I'm going to get that string from the prees' room, and tie the end of their bed-clothes together. *Someone* will lose her sheets and blankets unexpectedly tonight!''

There was a smothered giggle as they pictured the dismay

124

of the girls when they found their bed-clothes mysteriously gone, but Joey hushed them at once.

"We'll powder Signa's and Ilonka's baths with fizzy stuff," she said, when all was quiet again. "I looked at the bath-list before coming up, and they are first out of that dormy to-morrow. They'll think something's happened when the water all bubbles up. I've got a tin of stuff I'm supposed to take sometimes — here it is. It'll do the trick beautifully, and they'll imagine the whole place is bewitched or something."

"Cyrilla and Liebchen still remain," said Frieda.

"Well, I'm not just sure about those two. They *might* have joined in. On the other hand, they mightn't. Anyway, we'll do the others first, and then see."

No sooner said than done. Frieda divided the cornflour with Simone, and the pair crept into the Green dormitory and managed to powder the four people chosen for this punishment without disturbing any of the others, though a drowsy murmur coming from Margia's cubicle turned them cold with horror for a moment. Luckily, Margia was not really wakened, and she turned over — they could hear her — and sank back into deep slumber again.

Scarcely daring to breathe, Frieda and Simone got back to their friends, to find that Joey had the string ready, and Marie had gone to the bathroom, and was busy powdering the baths. Jo stole into the Green dormitory, and fastened the string to the bed-clothes as she had arranged. In one way, she had by far the most dangerous task to perform, for both Margia and Suzanne slept very lightly as a rule, and the string had to be taken across the floor of Suzanne's cubicle and under the curtains before it was tied to Margia's bed-clothes. However, it was safely accomplished, and when Joey sped back, it was to find that Marie had finished the baths. Also, Frieda and Simone, inspired to deeds of daring by what had gone before, had decided to duplicate the string idea with Cyrilla and

125

Liebchen, and, having got another ball of string from the prefects' room, had gone to perform the deed.

Finally they all got back to their own dormitory and tumbled into bed with the feeling of having accomplished something worth mentioning.

It was nearly six o'clock when Joey, who slept as lightly as Margia and Suzanne, was wakened by a yell from downstairs. She guessed at once what had happened, and longed to be able to communicate her guess to Frieda or Simone or Marie. She dared not, however; but she lay chuckling at the thoughts of Margia's — it was Margia she had heard — indignation when she found out what had happened. She fell asleep again, still chuckling, and never awoke till Mary came into her cubicle and asked if she meant to sleep all day. The bell for *Früstück* would ring in ten minutes' time, and she would be late.

"Get up, Jo," went on Mary authoritatively. "You'll have to rush as it is, and you said that Dr Jem said you could keep school-hours now."

"Wish Jem would mind his own business!" grumbled Joey, dragging her black eyes open with an effort. "Don't see why we should get up so early on Sundays at all!"

This from Joey, who was famed for waking at unearthly hours as a rule, so surprised Mary that she had nothing to say. Then she wondered if perhaps Jo was still feeling the effects of her illness, so she suggested that she should go and ask Mrs Russell if the other girl might stay in bed a little longer.

That brought Jo out of bed with a bound. She had no desire for Madge to hear of her unaccountable sleepiness, for that lady was gifted in the art of putting two and two together, and in this case they would make an uncomfortable four for Miss Joey. So she got up and made for the bathroom with all speed. On the way she encountered Deira, who was coming upstairs, laughing all the way.

"What's the joke?" demanded Jo.

Deira looked at her solemnly. "So you did it after all, you monkey?" she said. "Sure, those middles are furious! They made such a noise over their hair gone white in a single night that I had to go in to them, or Matron would certainly have heard them, and *then* where would you have been, my pretty colleen?"

"In the soup!" said Jo frankly.

"So I thought. You're a mad set, all of you! And I suppose it was you who tied Margia's and Suzanne's bed-clothes together, and gave them both such an unpleasant awakening early this morning? Oh, you needn't pretend! I've heard all about it from them!"

Jo would have asked what she had heard, but the sound of footsteps lower down convinced her that discretion was the better part of valour just now. She tore down the few remaining stairs and slammed the bathroom door shut. Her bath was, as she said after, "a cat's lick and a promise," and dressing was a sketchy affair. Thanks to the kindness of Mary and Frieda, she was ready in time, and her bed opened to air, but it was a scramble, and she felt breathless when she went down with the others.

In the *Speisesaal*, Cornelia and Evadne eyed them malignantly. They had brushed and brushed at their hair, and all the corn-flour wasn't out yet, even though Frieda and Simone had only been able to dust it on lightly. Yvette and Anita, who had long dark manes, looked decidedly grey still, and *they* glared at Jo and her gang when they entered the room. The middles had no trouble in fixing the blame for their fright of that morning where it was deserved.

"You *are* pigs!" hissed Evadne at them as she passed them. "Say! You can bet your bottom dollar we'll pay you out, the lot of you!"

She had to go to her own seat after this, and Jo grinned at her pleasantly from the seniors' table. Evadne met the grin with

127

a scowl, but that only pleased the wicked four still more. It was a good thing for them that the prefect on duty at the middles' table was Deira that morning. Mary would have found things out in a minute, and, in her present frame of mind, would certainly have reported the matter.

Still, safe though they might imagine themselves to be, they were not as safe as they thought, and retribution was to fall on them before the day was out.

CHAPTER FIFTEEN

Retribution

After breakfast everyone rushed upstairs to make her bed, for once that was done, what time came between bed-making and service was their own. The members of the Yellow dormitory did their work as quickly as possible, for Mary had letters to write and the other five wanted to discuss what had happened in school during Jo's absence. The middles belonging to the Blue and Green dormitories also hurried. *They* wanted to settle on a plan for revenging themselves on the Yellows for the shocks they had all received that morning. Margia and Suzanne especially, who had been wakened at the early hour of six to find their bed-clothes mysteriously disappearing, were indignant. Joey had made her string as tight as possible, drawing it taut, so that the cubicle curtains were raised on it, and this additional weight had done all she could have desired for the pair.

As for the four who had been powdered, the first to discover it had been Yvette, who happened to be up first. Her squall of horror when she saw herself in the mirror with white locks had roused all the other seven most effectively, and had brought in Deira from the next-door dormitory to see what on earth they were doing. None of the staff interfered, for the prefects and Matron were supposed to be responsible for the dormitories last thing at night and before breakfast. Matron had gone to Hilda Bhaer in the Violet dormitory because that young lady had awakened up complaining of feeling sick, and she had taken no notice of the uproar in the Green dormitory, knowing that the prefects from the Orange room would go to the rescue.

In this she was quite right, for Deira had gone over at once, and then had stood stock-still, silent from the shock of seeing four middles whose front hair had unaccountably turned white in a night. She had guessed almost immediately what had happened, of course, and she was able to calm their fears — though not their rage — once they found what had really happened; and then wild yells from bathrooms A and B had warned her of fresh pranks, and she had gone to the rescue, murmuring to herself, "Isn't Jo the limit?"

By the time she had succeeded in persuading Signa and Ilonka that magic had *not* been practised on them, and that there was nothing poisonous in the water, the three of them had to hurry to get ready in time. As for Cyrilla and Liebchen, Frieda and Simone had not done their work nearly so effectively as Joey, and they had discovered nothing wrong till Cyrilla, who was dressed first, went to throw back the clothes from her bed. Then she discovered that she was also removing Liebchen's, while Liebchen nearly shrieked in terror when she saw her sheets and blankets going for a walk by themselves, and with nothing — so far as she could see — to account for it. Everyone was very angry, and especially Anita and Yvette, who had brushed and brushed their hair before breakfast and were still grey on top. They set to work again with brushes and combs — but still the obstinate cornflour would *not* come out.

"There'll be such a fuss if Madame catches you like that!" said Margia gloomily, as she eyed Yvette's long dark tresses. "Wonder why it sticks to *your* hair? Evvy and Cornelia have got it out all right."

"That's all you know," said Evadne. "My hair's still full of it. But it shows more on dark hair, of course. Corney's all right — hers is so fair that it didn't show that much this morning; and I'm not too bad — to look at! But Yvette's is dark brown and Anita's *black*, and it looks simply *awful* on them!"

Awful it did look! The afflicted pair brushed and brushed, and then the others took it in turns to do what they could. Finally Matron came and sent them downstairs, for the stove was allowed to go out during the day and the room was getting cold.

"We've done our best," said Margia despairingly, "but there's no getting away from it that it's clear *something* has happened to you both! Joey and the others are utter rotters to have done a thing like this!"

"Slang, Margia!" said an unexpected voice behind them. "I am surprised at you!"

The four wheeled round, Margia and Cornelia keeping as much in front of the other two as possible. Unfortunately, Yvette was a tall child, and half a head above the two Americans. Mrs Russell glanced at her and then uttered an exclamation of horror. "Yvette! Come into the light at once!"

Catching Yvette by the arm she pulled her into the study, where, in the full white glare that came through the windows, she saw all that there was to be seen. The others had followed, not knowing what else to do, and the mistress at once called them in and examined their hair. Margia was all right, but Evadne still showed traces of cornflour, and Anita was nearly as bad as Yvette.

"Well?" said Mrs Russell, when she had finished.

No one said anything. Evadne rubbed the toe of her right slipper up and down her left leg, an exercise to which she was addicted when in an awkward position; Anita twisted her fingers together and looked down at them; the other two sought inspiration from the ceiling — and failed to find it.

"Well?"

The icy syllable reminded them that they had kept their old Head waiting for an answer.

"I — think that we've got a — a little — flour in our hair," faltered Evadne at last.

"Is this meant to be funny?" demanded Mrs Russell.

"N-no-o-o," said Evadne ruefully.

"Did you do it yourselves?"

"Oh no, Madame!" Yvette assured her in heartfelt accents.

131

"Do you know anything about it, Margia?"

"No, Madame," said Margia.

"I see." There was a pause, during which Evadne did her best to rub a hole in her stocking, and the other three squirmed about uneasily. Then Mrs Russell asked, "Is anyone else powdered?"

"Yes — Cornelia," said Margia.

"Go and bring her, Margia."

Margia went off, and presently returned with Cornelia. The Head looked at her hair and found it like Evadne's. But they had got off lightly, for their cropped locks had made it an easy matter to brush out most of the stuff. The real sufferers were Yvette and Anita, whose heavy hair held the fine dust most effectively.

"I'm afraid you two will have to be shampooed," said Mrs Russell to them. "Don't worry about it though. You won't have to do it yourselves, and you won't even have to *dry* it yourselves. I am sorry this has happened on a Sunday, but it must be done at once, or it will be twice as difficult to get out. Go and ring the bell, Margia, and tell everyone to go into the hall and wait there till I come. You four — Evadne, Cornelia, Yvette, and Anita — will wait here with me."

Margia went off, wishing she had held her tongue, and rang the bell as desired. The girls crowded into the passage, demanding to know the reason for it.

"It isn't church time yet!" protested Mary.

"I know. But Madame wants everyone in the hall, and we're to wait there till she comes. Tell them, Mary," said Margia.

Mary raised her voice at once. "Girls, you are all to go to the hall! Madame wants to speak to us."

The girls turned, and at once made for the narrow covered passage that led to the hall. Most of them wondered what in the world was the meaning of this sudden summons; but four faces fell at once, and Joey, Frieda, Simone, and Marie took their seats in a gloomy silence.

Silence fell on the room when the door opened and Mrs Russell marched in, followed by Cornelia, Evadne, Yvette and Anita. There was a look on her face which reminded those who had been there to see it of a day during the first term of the Chalet School when Grizel Cochrane had been misguided enough to vaseline all the blackboards.

"Oh my hat!" Joey murmured to Frieda. "We're for it this time!"

Mrs Russell mounted the little platform at the end of the hall, signing to the four middles to stand beneath.

"Someone has powdered with flour, or something else of that kind, the hair of these four girls," she said, coming to the point at once. "Will the girl who was responsible stand up at once!"

Frieda, Simone, Joey, and Marie all rose with scarlet faces.

"*You*?" exclaimed the startled Head. "*You* four?"

The whole school stared at them.

"Stand out!" the Head commanded.

They moved out of their seats and stood before her.

"What have you to say for yourselves?" she demanded.

"It — it was only a joke," mumbled Joey, after a pause.

"A joke? You, a prefect, consider such childish silliness a *joke*?"

"'Twas me who thought of it," said Simone suddenly.

"And I helped to do it," added Frieda.

The Head looked at them coldly. Then she turned to Marie. "And what hand had you in the matter, Marie?"

"I — supported them," faltered Marie.

Margia jumped up from her seat. "Please, Madame, if you come to that, we asked for it!" she announced.

Mrs Russell stared as if unable to believe her ears. "What do you mean, Margia?"

"We-ell," began Margia, "we played a joke on them, and — I suppose — this — was a — a sort of — pay-back," she concluded very lamely, and then stood as scarlet as the others.

Mrs Russell's face lost some of its severity. As a matter of fact she was on the verge of laughter, but she could not let the girls know that. So, with an effort, she pulled her lips into straight lines and surveyed the girls in silence. "And who else was in this?" she asked.

The members of the Green and Blue dormitories stood up, all blushing in various degrees. There was another silence, during which Joey and the other three wished devoutly that the floor would open and swallow them up.

Finally the Head spoke again. "Thank you," she said. "Beyond saying that you middles are even more babyish than I had thought, I will say nothing further."

It was quite enough. People of thirteen and fourteen object to being called 'babyish,' and the word, uttered in Madame's cool, cutting tones, hurt. The middles sat down, wishing they had never thought of playing practical jokes on the seniors, and Madge turned her attention to her young sister and her gang. "Did you forget that you are prefects?" she asked chillingly.

"Subs," murmured Joey.

But Madge heard her. "As you remind me, Josephine — *sub*-prefects; therefore on trial for positions as full prefects. And do you consider that your behaviour has been suitable for prefects, whether full or sub?"

She got no answer to *that* question. No one had any to make.

"If I called the middles babyish," she went on, "I can only say of you that you are infantile. As there seems to have been some provocation for your foolish acts, I will not punish you further this time than to say that as you have caused the trouble, you must undo it as far as possible. Instead of being free this afternoon, you four will shampoo — and *thoroughly* — the hair of these four girls; and then dry it." She waited a moment to let this sink in; then she dismissed them and retired to the study and her son, who sat up among his cushions and stared solemnly

134

at his mother when she flung herself into a chair and gave way to peals of laughter.

"It was very naughty of them," said Mademoiselle, who had come in and caught her.

"Very naughty indeed," agreed Madge. "Oh, Thérèse! Did you see their faces when they heard about the shampooing? I nearly collapsed then and there."

Just then a tap at the door was followed by the entrance of Mary, suffering from a bad-conscience attack, and she had come to Mrs Russell to confess her misdeeds at once.

The young Head listened to her gravely, and spoke very seriously to her about the obligations under which she, as head-girl of the school, lay; but she sent Mary away happy once more, and with a mind completely at rest.

"If we are going to have any more alarms and excursions while I am here," observed Mrs Russell, "I shall begin to think that it is my influence."

CHAPTER SIXTEEN

The Amnesty is Broken

The middles, and those four prefects who had been responsible for the mischief done in the dormitories remained subdued for three days, after which human nature reasserted itself and they were natural once more.

None of the eight people concerned would be likely to forget that shampooing. Frieda and Simone, as the two who had done the powdering, had to take on Yvette and Anita, and the labour of clearing the long, thick, slightly oily hair of cornflour was not a light one. Joey and Marie had Cornelia and Evadne to attend to, and as both wriggled violently nearly all the time, the shampooers had their work cut out not to make a mess in the bathrooms.

Halfway through the business, Joey was moved to wonder aloud if water mixed with cornflour would result in some kind of blancmange. Cornelia, to whom she had made the remark, twisted away from the basin at once, and, regardless of the dripping soap making a mess on the floor, dashed to the mirror to see. Jo, grabbing her firmly by the shoulder, had her back in her place in a moment, but not before the spotless linoleum was speckled with blobs of lather in all directions; and the prefect held her tongue for the rest of the operation, till she had Cornelia safely in the Fourth form-room before the stove, in company with Evadne, whose hair Marie was solemnly rubbing with a towel.

It took the whole afternoon, and no one had time for anything else before the bell rang for *Kaffee und Kuchen*, which they had, as usual, in the big form-room, which belonged to whichever form held the largest number of girls. This year it was the Third, which numbered twenty to the Fourth's ten.

Mary was at the big urn that held the milky coffee they all drank here, and Deira, Vanna, Carla, and a pretty Polish girl, Natasha Patrovska, were handing round the cakes and twists of sweet bread that always accompanied it. The eight scattered to their own clans, and Joey sank into a low basket-chair with a sigh of relief.

The Robin, who had been sitting beside Mary's smallest sister, Peggy, jumped up and ran across to her. "You have been so long, Joey!" she said, snuggling down on her adored Jo's knees.

"Well, Cornelia wriggles so!" said Joey, slipping an arm round her. "What have you been doing this afternoon, *mein Vöglein*?"

"I wrote my letter to papa," said the Robin, "and then Peggy and I made a puzzle. Then Miss Nalder came and read to us."

Joey accepted her coffee from Frieda, who had brought it with her own. Deira produced cakes, and when they were all supplied, they settled down to talk of the Saints.

"As we have called off the feud business, I think we ought to do something for them," said Jo.

"What?" asked Mary.

"Oh, a bean-feast or some kind or other! What about a musical evening?"

"I daresay!" protested Margia. "Then you can wriggle out of playing!"

"Jo could *not* wriggle out, as you say," said Simone with dignity. "She would not play, but she would sing."

"Of course she would!" put in Mary hastily, for she saw an argumentative look on Margia's face, and Simone was easily upset. "It's rather a good idea, Joey — especially if Grizel is coming and bringing with her another pianist. With them, and Margia, and Frieda's harp, and Deira's violin, and Lilli's cello, and singing from you and Cornelia and Jeanne le Cadoulec, we could get up a pretty decent programme, I should think."

"The Robin can sing, too," said Joey.

"I will sing 'The Red Safaran', Joey," cried Robin.

"Well, what about it, Mary?" said Joey.

Everyone looked at Mary eagerly to see what she did think about it, and everyone was satisfied when she nodded and said, "I'll go and see Madame and Mademoiselle tomorrow. If they agree, I think it would be snappy."

However, things were not to be so easy as that. As it was a fine night, the Saints walked round the lake to the Chalet for evensong, held by Mr Eastley in the little chapel, while the Catholics went to Benediction in the tiny white-washed church which served the whole valley. The priest had to ministrate to several others round the lake, and Briesau had him only once in three weeks. This was his Sunday there, and the girls were expected to make the most of it.

In the little chapel belonging to the school, besides the Saints and the odd twenty or so members of the Church of England that were among the girls of the Chalet School, as well as the staff from both schools, there were Dick Bettany, who had been up to the Sonnalpe for the week, and had run down with Dr Jem for the Sunday with his twin; Dr. Maynard, who could be spared from the sanatorium, since there were no very bad cases at present; and the English Consul from one of the South Tyrol towns, who was snatching a week's leave and had come to the Tiernsee for skating. It was a bright little service, with plenty of hymns, which the girls all liked, one lesson, and a short sermon by the clergyman. Dick and the Consul acted as sidesmen, and took the collection, which, like most of their efforts at nights, would go to the free ward of the sanatorium. Service being over, the girls wandered out to the hall, where the visitors lingered for a short chat about various interests they had in common.

It was at this time that Elaine Gilling, who since the accident that had so nearly cost them the lives of Joey and Maureen had been much quieter, took it upon herself to say to Mary Burnett,

138

in the presence of Joey Bettany, the Robin - the Catholic girls had come in by his time - and Evadne Lannis, "It's all very well, but I do think *we* might have have some say in the collections!"

"How do you mean?" demanded Joey.

"Well, where they're to go, and so on. It's always what you Chalet people say, and as we are a much bigger number than you, I don't think it's fair."

"But what do you want to do with them?" asked Mary.

"Well, why shouldn't they go to foreign missions sometimes?" asked Elaine.

"Such as which?" queried Joey, with a grin. "You mustn't forget that we aren't all English here. Some of our girls are Americans, and some are Germans and Norwegians. It's only because this is the only form of Protestant religion hereabouts that they all come to this. And you can't expect them to feel any interest in the SPG or the YMCA"

"In any case," added Mary sensibly, "I think we ought help those near at hand, and that means the lake poor and the san."

The Robin took a hand. "We have a bed in the ward for little children," she said, lifting her dark eyes to the elder girl's face. "It's a free ward, you know, and we send money each year to keep one bed for a little girl who is ill of the same illness that killed my mamma. If you of St. Scholastika's sent money for a bed, too, then you would like to send your collections to the sanatorium, would you not?"

She laid a hand on Elaine's arm in her eagerness, but Elaine had never been friends with herself since that day when her own temper and negligence had brought about what might so nearly have been a tragedy. She blamed the Chalet girls for her discomfort, and the Robin's childish appeal brought no answer from her. Instead, she flung off the little hand so roughly that the child staggered and caught at Joey to save herself from falling. Jo, furious at the school-baby being treated so, steadied her, and then, with an arm round the little shoulders, said, "I can *quite* understand that *you* don't care what happened to sick children! How dare you treat the Robin like that?"

Secretly, Elaine was ashamed of herself, but she wasn't going to say so - not likely! And least of all to Joey Bettany. She shrugged her shoulders. "I didn't hurt the kid; she's all right. The fact of the matter is, she's thoroughly spoiled! As for that blessed san you all think so much of, the people have priests and so on up there, and I think that church collections should be given to the church."

"Robin *isn't* spoiled!" cried Mary indignantly. "She's the least spoiled child I've ever known! As for the collections, our chaplain is Mr Eastley, and *he* has most right to say where the money should go. It was his own arrangement that the morning money should go to the poor here, and the evening to the san! And if you don't like our arrangements, get a chapel of your own, and don't come here finding fault with ours!"

Elaine turned away with a sneer on her face, and Mary and Joey directed their attention to the Robin, who was absolutely bewildered. She hadn't meant any harm when she had put her hand on Elaine's arm, and the rough treatment puzzled her. Spoiled, she certainly was *not*; but petted she had been nearly all the nine years she had lived.

"Was I naughty, Joey," she asked. "I never meant to be."

"No, darling," said Jo tenderly. "You weren't naughty at all. Don't think any more about it. See, Miss Durrant is coming to take you over to Le Petit Chalet. Kiss me 'good-night'."

The Robin held up her face for good-night kisses.

Jo and Mary were wildly indignant at the treatment meted out to the school-pet. As luck would have it, Margia, Evadne and Suzanne had seen what had happened, and they, too, were angry. The story lost nothing in the telling, and by the next morning had swelled to terrific proportions. Madge was electrified to hear - from Kitty Burnett, who was a heedless young person who said exactly what came into her head — that last night, the big girl from St. Scholastika's had grabbed the Robin by the arm and shaken her till she couldn't stand, and then had a stand-up fight with Joey and Mary!

The Head had more sense than to accept this rigmarole, but she knew that there is no smoke without fire, so she summoned Mary and Joey to the study and asked them what it meant. "Of course, I know that it has been exaggerated," she said. "At the same time, I should like to have your versions of the affair. Was Elaine really so unkind to the Robin? If so, I must lodge a complaint with Miss Browne."

"Elaine didn't do that, Madame," said Mary. The Robin took hold of her arm, and she shook her off. I don't suppose she meant to be rough, but — "

Joey broke in here. "Didn't mean to be rough? Then what *did* she mean? She made the kid nearly come a cropper, anyway. She *would* have fallen if I hadn't been there to catch her! It was nothing but nasty temper, and jealousy 'cos we're a better school than they are! That's the whole truth of the matter!"

Madge looked at her consideringly. "Are we a better school? I am not so sure when you talk like that, Josephine. Once and for all, I will not permit this use of slang, and if I have to complain of your language again, I must punish you severely. It was bad enough when you were a middle. Now that you are a senior and a sub-prefect, it is worse than that. Also, I do not like the spirit of your words. What right have you to say that Elaine meant to be rough?"

Thus pulled up in her stride, Joey had nothing further to say, and Mary finished explaining exactly what had happened without any further interruption from her impulsive friend.

Mrs Russell looked serious over the matter. It wasn't the treatment of the Robin that was troubling her at the moment, though she was rather shocked to think that any girl of seventeen could treat another so much smaller than herself in that way.

But it showed her that the feeling between the two schools was anything but what it ought to be, and she feared that the incident would make matters worse. "I suppose everyone knows of this?" she said.

"I should think so," agreed Mary. "Some of the middles were standing near, and saw, and they will have spread it all over by this time. Elaine is the girl who is most bitter against us, Madame, said Mary. Some of them seemed anxious to be friendly; but she seems to hate us."

Madge lifted a worried face. "I am sorry to hear this," she said gravely.

Jo spoke up. "I think, Madame, that it's because Elaine got into such trouble over that ice affair that she hates us. You see, Gipsy told me that some of them begged her to put a stop to it, and she wouldn't. She knows that it was her fault that Maureen has been so ill, and — and has — has — " Joey ran down, not being very sure how to word her ideas.

Madge sat back, looking at her. "There is a good deal in that, Jo," she said quietly. "I am sorry for Elaine, if that is the case, for we can do nothing."

"There's another reason," said Mary. "We have Guides and they haven't. Elaine is dying to be a Guide, but Miss Browne doesn't approve of them."

Madge thought this very probable. Elaine was just the type of girl to need all that the Guides could have given her.

She was silent again for a while. Then, feeling that there was, at present, no way out of this, she told the girls that they might go, but, in the meantime, they were not to mention the affair again, and they were to suppress anyone whom they heard talking about it.

But Elaine had made mischief again, and the middles were determined that the big girl's treatment of the Robin should not go unpunished.

CHAPTER SEVENTEEN

Chicken-Pox

"Snow again!" cried Joey, when she looked out of her window the next morning. "Well, all I can say is that I hope everyone is satisfied with the amount of snow we are getting this year! If it goes on much longer, we'll all be buried alive!"

"And this is only November," Mary reminded her, as she tumbled out of bed. "Oh, bother! No walks today, and the middles are simply spoiling for trouble!"

"They'd better!" Joey squatted on the floor to put on her stockings. "I say, Mary, don't you think we might rehearse today? Plato won't be coming if the weather's like this, and I doubt if Herr Anserl will get up."

"Good idea," said Mary. "Frieda Mensch! Do you mean to get up today or tomorrow?"

There was a voice from Frieda's corner, uttering a groan. Then, "I wish I could stay in bed today. I feel so shivery."

"*Frieda*!". Mary made a dive for her cubicle, and Joey followed, only to be turned back. Mary felt the Austrian girl's hands, looked at her face, which was certainly flushed, and finally said, "You'd better stay where you are. You're a bit hot, anyhow." Then she went back to her cubicle to slip on her dressing-gown and bedroom slippers, and then away to summon Matron.

Meanwhile the other three were dressing at top speed, talking to Frieda all the time.

"Got a sore throat?" asked Joey genially, as she brushed her hair vigorously.

"Know what's wrong with you?" added Marie.

"No," returned Frieda, answering both questions at once. "But I feel so sick, and I have such a pain!"

"P'r'aps it's appendicitis," suggested Jo thoughtfully.

"I do not think so," said Frieda, not alarmed by this pronouncement, since she knew Jo.

"I am hot and thirsty, and I ache all over."

"Flu for a ducat, then!"

At this point Matron came in, looking grim. It was just as well, for at Jo's last pronouncement, Frieda had begun to cry weakly. She really felt very poorly, and her back and head were aching badly. Matron took her temperature, felt her pulse, looked at her tongue and throat, and then, after pulling the bed straight, and turning the pillow, told her she might stay where she was for the present, at any rate. "You others leave the room," she continued. "I must see Madame about this."

"What's up with Frieda?" demanded Joey, as she turned to obey.

"Cold," said Matron sharply. "Do as I tell you, Jo, and don't stand there arguing!"

Jo marched out of the room, but she was by no means satisfied, and she confided her ideas to the others when they reached the prefects'-room, where they found Deira and Carla already at work — a new rule, instituted that term, had given the girls half an hour's prep before breakfast and shortened their evening work. "It's my belief," she said, as she opened her *Virgil*, "that Frieda has something infectious."

"Nonsense, Jo!" said Mary. "In that case, *we* should have been quarantined too, and not sent down here to work as usual."

As if to contradict this statement, the door opened at this moment and Matron appeared. "Are all you prefects here? Where is Vanna? Who else is in the Sixth besides you?"

"Only Natasha," said Jo.

"She practises at this time, doesn't she?" went on Matron. "Run and tell her that I want her, Marie. No, Jo; not you. You are not to run about the passages any more than can be helped. Do try to remember that you are expected to take care of yourself just now. You will be sixteen in a few days' time; try to behave as though you *were* sixteen!"

Marie got up, and went away to return presently with Natasha, who looked surprised.

"Where have you been practising?" demanded the domestic tyrant.

"In music-room B," replied the Polish girl.

"Have you been with any of the others?"

"But no, Matron. I went straight to the piano, and have seen no one till Marie came."

"Then *that's* all right," said Matron, drawing a long breath. "Marie, go and lock the door of the music-room and bring the key here to me. And understand, girls, that you are not to leave this room till I say so. I will bring your breakfast up here myself, and someone will come to you presently.

"But, Matron, why?" asked Mary.

"I don't like Frieda's looks. It strikes me we are in for something infectious — chicken-pox, I think. She tells me that she has never had it. How many of you people have?"

"I had it years ago when I was a small kid," said Joey.

"So had I," said Mary.

Carla and Marie had both had it, but none of the others, so far as they knew, had suffered from it.

Joey, as usual, promptly thought of a side-issue. "What about Bernhilda's wedding? It comes off in six weeks' time. Will Frieda be all right by then?"

"Of course she will," snapped Matron, who was worried and anxious. "How long do you imagine it lasts? It won't even be a bad case, though she feels miserable just now."

She turned to leave the room, but the door opened once more, and Miss Maynard entered, looking disturbed. "Ah, there you are, Matron. Madame would like to see you at once."

"Miss Maynard, Frieda's got chicken-pox — Matron *thinks*!" cried Joey.

Miss Maynard groaned. "So it *has* come, then! Oh! And we were hoping that perhaps we should escape after all!"

Jo opened her eyes, and the rest raised interested faces at this remark.

"They have it at St. Scholastika's," explained Miss Maynard. "Miss Browne has just rung up Madame to tell her, and to warn us to keep a lookout for it."

Matron bustled out after this, leaving the senior-mistress with the girls.

"Many of them down?" asked Mary.

"Seven," said Miss Maynard.

"Well, I think they might have kept it to themselves," observed Joey indignantly. "It's going to mess up the rest of the term!"

"We'll hope not," said the mistress.

"You'll see! It just will! Our play won't come off, and we'll all be stopped going to Bernhilda's wedding, and most of us will have to spend Christmas here, too!" was the pessimistic response.

"*You* won't; you've had it already," said Mary. "So have I; and so have Carla and Marie."

"But we have not had it," wailed Simone.

"Sure?" asked Miss Maynard.

"I do not remember it," said Simone dejectedly.

"Cheer up, Simone. You may have had it too young for that. We shall soon find out from your parents."

When Miss Maynard had left the room, the prefects looked at each other mournfully.

"All this term messed up!" repeated Joey.

"It is just like those Saints!" put in Deira. "I wish they'd never come here!"

"I also!" agreed Marie devoutly.

It was the general feeling, but it didn't make much difference to the fact that, if it was really chicken-pox that Frieda had

146

caught, the end of the term would be spoilt.

A little cry suddenly escaped Joey. "David! He's here — right in the middle of it. Oh, whatever will Madge do?"

The girls looked at each other. Mrs Russell's small son was adored by them all. He was a happy chuckling baby, very like his mother in looks, and ready to go to anyone. Only the day before Frieda had been nursing him, and now she was down with chicken-pox!

Joey jumped to her feet, and made for the door.

"Jo! Where are you going?" cried Mary.

"To my sister! I must see her at once!"

Before anyone could speak, impulsive Joey was flying downstairs to the study where the two Heads were sitting at the desk and table respectively, writing notes to the different parents to ask if the girls had had chicken-pox, and if not, what was to be done with them. They both looked up startled when the tall girl came rushing in.

"Jo!" cried Madge.

Jo tumbled down in a heap at her sister's feet, coughing with breathlessness, and Madge had to leave her till she was fit to answer. Mademoiselle left the room, and presently came back with a glass of water. By that time Joey was sitting in a chair, looking white and exhausted by her bad fit of coughing. Madge took the water, and gave her a little of it.

Presently Joey looked up. "Madge! What about Davie?"

Madge whitened a little. She had been trying not to think about it. But she spoke quite steadily. "I have sent for Jem. He will tell us what to do. Jo, you must *not* run about like this. Don't you think I have had enough worry with you as it is?"

"I'm sorry," murmured Joey.

Her sister sat down beside her and told her their plans as far as they had gone — which wasn't very far.

"Frieda has it, I am afraid, from what Matron says. We have asked all the girls, and while some of them know that they have

147

had it, others aren't sure; and others either don't know at all or else are certain that they've never had it. For today, there will be no lessons. Those of you whom we know to be safe will be sent out for a walk in one direction, while the doubtful ones will go in another, and those who are certain they have never had chicken-pox will go in a third. At least, you will all be in the open air, which is the best thing possible. You will be separated for all meals, and I am going to have the dormitories rearranged. The juniors will be completely kept apart from you, and the Robin and David are going up to the Sonnalpe as soon as possible. Davie is far too young to be allowed to run any risks, and you know what we feel about the Robin.''

''Righto!'' said Jo. ''And - what about the rest of us?''

''That, we have not yet decided,'' replied Madge.

While she had been speaking the door had opened, and a slight, graceful girl, with laughing grey eyes and beautifully shingled head, had come quietly in. It was Grizel Cochrane — last term's head-girl — come from Florence to spend her vacation at the school she loved so well, and turned up just when they did *not* want her!

Behind her was a much taller girl. Joey guessed this to be the Gerry Challoner of Grizel's last letter, and, as it turned out, she was right.

''Hello,'' said Grizel. ''We got here latish last night, so we put up at 'The Post' till this morning, and then I brought Gerry — this is her — and came to surprise you. We put our things in the cloak-room, and came here. But you don't seem awfully pleased to see us,'' she added, looking puzzled.

''*Pleased*!'' exclaimed Madge. ''If anything was wanted to put the finishing stroke to things, it's your arrival at this moment!''

Grizel stared, while Gerry Challoner looked uncomfortable. Joey decided that this was where she had better take a hand, and got up from her chair. ''Hello, Griselda,'' she said. ''We've got chicken-pox."

"*Who* has?" demanded Grizel.

"Well, Frieda, to be strictly accurate; but probably lots more who haven't had it already."

"Oh!" Grizel looked relieved. "Well, I've *had* it, so I can't get it again. What about you Gerry? Oh, by the way, I forgot. Madame, this is Gerry Challoner. Gerry, this is my Head-mistress, Mrs Russell, and her sister, Joey."

"Come and sit down," said Madge, with her charming smile. "I'm sorry to seem so inhospitable, but we've only just discovered that Frieda has chicken-pox, and things are rather at sixes and sevens."

"And I've had it," said Gerry.

"I am glad to know that," said her hostess. "Have you also had breakfast?"

"Half an hour ago. I routed them out, and made them give us coffee and rolls at half-past seven," explained Grizel. "We'll be glad of more, though, if we may. And, look here, Madame, can't we do something to help?"

"Yes, of course," said Gerry. "Do let us help you. I'm accustomed to crowds," she added, laughing, "though there *was* a time when I wasn't. But my guardian is a rector, and when I first went to live with them, there were ten at the Rectory, besides Uncle Arthur and Aunt Meg, and the maids. I was a prefect, too, of my form at the high school where I went, so I expect I could give you a hand all right."

"Ten children!" exclaimed Jo, before her sister could say anything. "Coo! Some family."

"I shall be glad of some help," said Madge, with brightening face. "Of course, Grizel was our head-girl only last term, and she knows our ways. You can help with some of the juniors, Grizel, for Miss Durrant and the rest of the staff will be busy. And if Miss Challoner will undertake to look after some of the middles for us, I shall be more than grateful!"

149

"Oh, rather," said Gerry. "But please don't call me 'Miss Challoner'. I'd much rather be 'Gerry' here, if I may."

Madge smiled at her. "I should like it. So 'Gerry' it shall be. Joey, you might take them upstairs to the prefects'-room for the present, and breakfast will be sent up there to you — or, rather, to all those who have had chicken-pox. Who are they? Have you any idea?"

"Mary, Carla, Marie, and me," said Jo promptly.

"What! Only for four of you? Haven't any of the others had it?"

"Simone doesn't know. Sophie, Vanna, Deira, and — no — I forgot — Frieda *has* it, now!"

Mademoiselle came back at that moment with some lists in her hands, and Madge turned to her at once. "Mademoiselle, has Simone had chicken-pox?"

"But yes. When she was only two," replied Mademoiselle. "And things are not so bad as they at first seemed, *chérie*. I find that there are only twenty of the girls who are certain they have not had it. The rest, some fifteen, are not sure, and everyone else had it quite young."

"Thirty-five out of seventy, then, to watch," said Madge. "And, of course, some of them may be quite safe. It's certainly better than I thought. Well, the thirty-five who have had it must have *Frühstück* in the *Speisesaal*, and the fifteen who are not sure can be in the prefects'-room. The rest may go to the Third form. Then, after that, everyone must bundle up and go out. Mercifully, it is a fine day, so they can stay out. The snow will give the middles plenty of fun, and the seniors too. By midday, we will have everything ready, and the local people will have let us know about their girls, so that will be some help. Run away now, girls, and remember that you are not to mix. Someone will come round while you are at breakfast and tell you about dressing arrangements, and so on." She smiled at them, and waved them off.

CHAPTER EIGHTEEN

The Battle

It was a funny morning, as Joey said afterwards when they were discussing it. After breakfast, where the tables seemed strangely denuded of their numbers, those who were safe were sent upstairs to their dormitories to get their things packed up in the trunks that had been brought down from the box-rooms while the girls were having their meal. Only the four people from the Green dormitory were not allowed to go. Matron saw to their belongings, and also saw drawers and cupboards that made her mentally resolve to institute reforms in the way of tidiness next term. However, there was no time for even scolding this morning, so she packed the trunks, and then went back to the sick-room where they had taken Frieda. After that the doubtfuls went, and then those who had never had it. Meanwhile, the safe girls had put on their outdoor things and gone out with Mary and Gerry in charge. No mistress could be spared, for all would have to help with the rearrangement of the dormitories. To make things easier, Mary went off on the road to Seehof with the nine senior girls and senior-middles who were left there, while Gerry, with Jo for company, took the rest of the middles. Of the twenty-one juniors, only seven were immune, and Grizel marched them off up to the pine-woods which clad the mountains, and there they had a fine time, making a snowman, with bits of black twig for eyes and nose and mouth.

The doubtfuls went out with Miss Nalder, after some discussion on the part of the staff. Those who were almost certain to get it were first inspected by Matron, who had armed herself with all the clinical thermometers the school possessed, and then all those who seemed in their normal health were sent out to the playing-field, to work off their superfluous energy there. Three middles and two juniors showed a point or two in temperature, and one of the middles — Ilonka Barkocz, complained of headache. These five were sent to the Green dormitory, where the stove was burning brightly and, later on, Ilonka was taken off to sick-room and put to bed.

At half-past eleven Jem arrived from the Sonnalpe and pronounced Frieda's case to be chicken-pox without a doubt. Ilonka, too, he thought, was likely to have it. The other four would have to be watched. He commended their arrangements; agreed that it would be best for David and the Robin to go to the Sonnalpe.

"Do you think Davie is likely to have it?" asked his wife.

"I hope not," he said, "but I'm afraid it's likely. But you needn't worry about him. He's a sturdy little rascal, and will be all right. It's the Robin that I'm anxious about. I had hoped we could keep her from anything of this kind for another five years or so. It's most unfortunate this should have happened now."

"Well, she'll be in the best place," said Madge. "You and Jack and Gottfried will all keep an eye on her, I know; and she will be right out of the danger-zone. Really, Jem, I do think this has been the most appalling term of all! First Joey nearly ends her own life through going after that wrong-headed Irish girl from St. Scholastika's. Then, just as we are getting over that, *this* starts! And, to wind up everything, Grizel turns up this morning, and a strange girl with her!"

Jem roared. "How like Grizel! Where are they now? Are they safe, by the way?"

"Oh, quite. Both had it when they were small, and they are out with the other safe girls. Grizel has the juniors over in the pine-wood; and Gerry Challoner has gone with the middles and Joey to the water-meadows at Seespitz. I couldn't spare any staff, you know. At least, Miss Nalder has the people we aren't sure about; but she was the only one I could send. The rest are all busy with beds and form-rooms. You see, everything will have to be rearranged, for I can't send the girls home till I hear from the parents."

"It will be the best thing if some of them go," pronounced Jem. "There's only another three weeks left of the term, in any case. However, as you say, you must wait till you hear from the parents before you do anything definite."

"And I *do* hope nothing further will happen before the end of term," said Madge, with a sigh.

"I don't suppose anything will," returned her husband, with an arm round her. "Don't go seeking trouble, dear, before it comes! Well, there isn't much that I can do just now, so I had better be getting back. One of us will be down every day for the next few days; and whoever comes tomorrow will take Davie and the Robin back, so have them ready, like a good girl. It's a blessing we have nothing special to worry about at the Sonnalpe just now."

"How is Mrs Eastley just now?" asked Madge.

"Better for the present," he said, a sudden shadow coming over his face. "Eastley is very bucked about her, poor chap."

The shadow was reflected in Madge's eyes. She knew that Mrs Eastley would never get well again, and that any improvement in her was only for the time being. Jem had warned her that the pretty little wife could not live many months longer, even in the health-giving air of the Sonnalpe. All they could hope to do was prolong her life a little, and keep her free from pain.

"If she had stayed in England," said the doctor gently, "she would have died weeks ago. Don't fret, Madge. He is a good chap, and when she leaves him he won't be without consolation."

Madge nodded, and then, as someone tapped at the door with a message for her, she turned away, and he gathered together his things and went off up the mountain to his work there.

It was midday before any of the girls came in, and then the people who had never had the illness were summoned to

153

Mittagessen, which they took in the Third form. After they had finished they were sent out again, and the doubtful girls were attended to in the prefects'-room, where they found things a decided crush, but all the more fun.

At one o'clock the safe people returned, and Madge had only to look at them to see that all had not gone well. Gerry Challoner's cheeks were scarlet, and some of the middles looked very downcast. The seniors seemed rather ashamed of themselves, too, though she couldn't imagine what had happened; and Grizel looked furious. "What has happened?" Madge demanded sharply.

"Ructions," said Joey shortly.

"What do you mean? What have you been doing, girls?"

There was no answer, and finally, Gerry had to come to the rescue. "We met some of the girls from St. Scholastika's, Mrs Russell," she said, "and they were — well — rather rude to our girls."

"*That* wasn't any excuse for our crowd," said Grizel gloomily.

"*What* happened?" Madge looked worried and perturbed. What could those wretched middles — she felt pretty sure that the middles had been in it — have been doing?

"A fight — of sorts," replied Grizel. "We were coming back, and caught them at it. I don't know how it all began, but Gerry does. We stopped it at once, and brought them back."

Madge thought for a moment. Then the sound of the telephone-bell decided her. "Go and get *Mittagessen*, girls," she said. "Grizel, will you take it, please? The staff have had theirs already. And Gerry, would you mind helping her? Thank you! Then, if you will come and see me when you have finished, perhaps I shall be better able to decide what to do."

She turned and went back to the study, where the telephone-bell was still ringing madly, and the culprits went off to change their outdoor things, and then to sit down to a good meal. When it was over, the girls were told to stay where they were and amuse themselves with books and puzzles till someone came to them. As they had had plenty of exercise, it had been decided that they should stay in for the afternoon. Grizel and Gerry, having seen them settled down, with the prefects present in charge, went off to the study, where Mrs Russell, having finished an omelette and some coffee, was waiting for them.

"What *has* happened?" she asked, before they were fairly inside the door. "Miss Browne was on the 'phone when the bell rang before *Mittagessen,* and she gave me such a muddled account of things that I really can't make out what actually occurred. Sit down and tell me all about it."

The two sat down, and when they were comfortable, Grizel looked at her ex-Head. "Why on earth did that school ever come here?" she demanded. "There isn't room for two, and from all I've seen today, I think the girls are little hooligans!"

"I gather that Miss Browne, the Headmistress, thought there *was* room for two," said Madge drily. "As for the girls, I don't suppose they are really any worse than some of ours."

"Oh, Madame! They *are*!" Grizel was up in arms at once.

"I think it really *was* more their fault than ours," said Gerry thoughtfully. "They seem to have such a grievance against the Chalet girls because of the church collections — though I don't really understand why."

Madge explained, and then asked her to go on.

"Well, when the middles had been snow-fighting for a while on that ground beside the inn — I forget its name — they came along and settled themselves in another part. Jo told me that she knew you wouldn't want our girls to mix with them because of the infection, so I called them together and told them not to go near the Saints, as they tell me they call them."

"Not much *saint* about them!" struck in Grizel. '*Demons*' would be a much better term!"

However, Madge silenced her with a wave, and Gerry went on:

"The Chalet people were really quite good. They kept to the boundary I gave them, and beyond calling *Guten Morgen* to some of them, they paid no attention. The Saints had no mistress with them — only a big girl, and presently she called them, and they all began to talk hard about something or other. I didn't worry much, and our girls were having a good time. Then, presently, some of the smaller Saints came near to us and began to shout — er — well 'Mingy beasts!' was one thing.''

Madge gasped. "And what did out girls do?" she asked, when she had recovered her breath.

"Some of them shouted back," said Grizel. "This was where *we* came on the scene.''

"I hope it was nothing rude?"

"About level," returned her old pupil briefly.

The Head groaned. "It *would* be! Evadne and Cornelia had a hand in it, of course?"

"Oh, they weren't the only ones. Evadne rose to some heights of language though!" And Grizel grinned in spite of herself.

Madge groaned again. She could imagine just to what heights Evadne had risen, and she wished she had managed to spare a mistress to take charge of the middles. After all, Gerry Challoner, though a very nice girl, she was sure, was a stranger to them, and she didn't look much older than Grizel.

"It wasn't anything outrageous," said Grizel comfortingly. "At least, it wasn't so bad as it might have been. Evadne's language can be an eye-opener on occasion. I *did* hear her addressing them as 'rubber-necked, splay-footed nincompoops,' but that was the worst. I think she lost her head."

"I hope someone spoke to her?" said Mrs Russell severely — secretly, she was dying to laugh. "I will not have the girls calling names at each other like so many little street arabs!"

"Oh yes," said Gerry cheerfully. "Joey crushed her most effectually. Unfortunately, someone threw a snowball — I never saw who it was, not which side — and that was the end of it.

They were all hard at it in less than two minutes, and it wasn't fun. There was downright malice behind it all."

"We kept Jo out of it," said Grizel. "I reminded her that if anything happened to her, you would be upset, and that there was quite enough to worry you. She stayed out, but she was mad about it. Then they started pelting us — and for all *they* knew, Gerry was a proper mistress."

"Or you either," said Madge, her lips setting in a straight line at this. "They know most of the girls quite well, and they knew that you two are not in the school. Well?"

"We got ours called off by degrees," said Gerry. "We took it in turns to grab one at a time, and remind her of what had been said, and send her over to Joey, who formed them into lines and kept them marching up and down. It was difficult work, because the Saints at first followed us up. Then they seemed to come to their senses a little, and they drew off. We got our girls into line, and walked them pretty briskly home. I think that is about all."

"And quite enough!" said the sorely harassed mistress.

"Well, it *was* their fault in the beginning," pointed out Grizel.

"There is very little consolation in that. I am ashamed to think that Chalet girls could behave so. There isn't any excuse for them, and I shall punish them all."

"The person who most wants punishing is that big girl of theirs," stated Grizel.

"I have no jurisdiction over girls from St. Scholastika's, Grizel. If they behave badly, their own mistresses must see to it. But I will not have our girls marring their own reputation. They will all be tired out after all that, and they may just go to bed for the rest of the day! Perhaps that will teach them to remember that Chalet girls have to behave like gentlewomen, whatever other girls may do!" She got up as she spoke, and left the room.

"Hard luck on Madame," said Grizel. "She's awfully

worried, of course, and this hasn't improved matters."

"Oh, they deserve a punishment," said Gerry easily. Her years at a big high school had taught her many things, and she was not disposed to blame the Head. "They've had their fun, and now they've got to pay for it. They've asked for trouble. But you never mentioned this other school to me, Grizel."

"I didn't know about it," explained Grizel. "I believe, now I come to think of it, that Jo did say something about it once when she wrote. But I didn't pay much attention."

They sat on in the cosy room, with the crackling of the wood in the stove and the 'tick-tock' of the clock as the only sounds. Both were tired with their morning's exercise, and Gerry, at least, was unaccustomed to the strong pure air. Presently the silence and warmth overcame them, and when the justly-incensed Head-mistress came back from administering a lecture she had never bettered, and sending to bed all those who had been in the fight of the morning, as well as one or two others who looked as though they would be better for the rest, she found that her guests were fast asleep.

She left them, after seeing that they were comfortable, and went off to consult with Matron and the staff as to the thousand-and-one arrangements that had to be made; packed David's and the Robin's belongings herself, in readiness for their trip to the Sonnalpe on the morrow; answered sundry telephone calls; and then saw to the stoves in the various rooms, since Hansi, whose work it was, was busy chopping wood and had a good many other tasks to finish.

Grizel and Gerry slept all the afternoon, and were very much ashamed of themselves when finally a call from St. Scholastika's woke them up.

"But I was so sleepy," apologised Grizel.

"It's the strong air," laughed Madge, as she took off the receiver. "I've put you both in the Blue dormitory, Grizel, if

158

you want to go and get ready for *Kaffee und Kuchen*. — Hello! Mrs Russell speaking.''

Seeing she was busy, the two girls went off to seek the Blue dormitory, and Madge settled down to hear an involved apology and explanation from Miss Browne, who had managed to extract some more of the story from her girls, and decided that they were to blame in the first instance.

CHAPTER NINETEEN

An Anonymous Letter

Bed for a whole day — just bed, with nothing to do but lie there and think over one's sins, so subdued the middles who had helped to make the trouble that, for the remaining three days of what had been the most troubled term of the Chalet School since it began, they were almost angelically good. By the Thursday morning most of the parents had replied to the notices sent out, and the majority had asked that their girls might be sent home.

"It's a relief," said Grizel to a select audience of Mary, Joey, Marie, Simone, and Gerry. "Those middles are angels just now, but it can't last long, and when the outbreak comes it's bound to be something awful to make up for present goodness. *I* know them!"

"Oh, middles are always a nuisance," said Gerry. "I know *we* were! What's going to happen to the people who aren't going home?"

"Maynie's taking six of them to Vienna," said Jo. "The rest are going to Salzburg with Miss Nalder. School will begin on the third of January, to make up for what we've missed this term. Easter term will be a fearful length, won't it?"

"But, Jo! And what of Bernhilda's wedding?" cried Marie, who, as sister of the bridegroom, considered this a most important event. "Frieda and I are to be her bridesmaids, and if we are at school, how can that be?"

"You can have a holiday, I suppose?" said Joey.

"But after returning to school so soon — will it be permitted?"

"Oh, bound to be! Bernie's asked all of us who were the first at the school to come, so they'll arrange things all right, you'll see," said optimistic Jo.

"What's that in your blazer-pocket?" demanded Grizel at this juncture.

Jo made a wild grab at her pocket and pulled out a letter. "What an ass I am! And I meant to tell you about it before! I've just had the most extraordinary letter from 'Veta. What she's driving at, I can't think! They must be giving her too many lessons, and she's suffering from softening of the brain."

"Oh, talk sense!" said Mary. "What does she say?"

Jo took the letter out of its envelope and smoothed out its numerous pages. Elisaveta, Crown Princess of Belsornia, wrote a big script hand which was clear to read, but, as Jo had once remarked, was hard on paper. The recipient of the letter now spread herself comfortably and read aloud:

"DEAR JOEY. — I've had such a funny letter from the Tiernsee. I cannot think what it all means, so I am writing to ask you.

"Do you know, Jo, I received a letter two days ago, and as it was postmarked Tiernsee they thought it came from someone at the Chalet, and gave it to me as usual. I thought it came from there, though I did not know the writing. But when I opened it and saw that Chalet School was not given as the address, but just Tiernsee, I began to wonder.

"Then I read it. Jo, it was the most startling letter! It said that I ought to know that a certain very common school at Briesau on the Tiernsee was claiming that I had been there for a time, and that the writer thought I ought to know about it. It went on that the girls called me by my name, without "Princess" in front of it — I should like to hear any of you people daring to call me "Princess"! There would be trouble if you did! — and that the writer felt that not only should I know this, but also my father; and she finished up by saying that she trusted that I would show this letter to him so that he might take steps to have it all stopped at once.

"Joey Bettany, is there a lunatic in the school? Or is it a silly joke on your part? If not, what *is* it? Please let me know by return of post, for I am dying to have the truth!

"The letter was not signed, except as "A Wellwisher," so I don't know who it is.

"Daddy and I both hope you are quite well again now. Madame sent me a post-card, to apologise for not answering my last letter to her, and on it she said that you had been very ill, but were getting better. What have you been doing? What was the matter with you, for I don't know that either. You people at the Tiernsee have neglected me shamefully these last few months! Even the Robin hasn't sent anything.

"Oh — sorry! Miss Burton said I was not to abbreviate words when I wrote letters, though why, I cannot see. That is why this one is so beautifully expressed!"

"And that's the most of it," concluded Joey, folding up the letter and returning it to its envelope. "But what do you think she means? *Has* anyone been writing letters to her like that as a silly joke? If so, who? 'Cos I must answer this as soon as poss! Poor 'Veta! We *have* been neglecting her! But why some of you idiots didn't write and tell her what was wrong, and all about Maureen and me, I can't think."

"We hadn't time to think of outside things," said Mary quietly. "As for that letter of which she speaks, I think it's fairly plain what has happened. Didn't some of the babes tell that wretched Elaine about her being here?"

"You did yourself," said Simone with interest. "And Joey told that one called Vera Smithers."

"Cornelia began it," said Jo, who was sitting on a chair-back at imminent risk of tilting over and collapsing on the stove. "I only chipped in when that wretched Vera kid said she didn't believe it and Cornelia was lying! Corney's an ass, but she's a truthful ass, and she was furious! So I just backed her up a bit. I wasn't putting on frills about it — not likely!"

"Well, I feel sure it's either Elaine or Vera," said Mary slowly.

"Choice crowd they seem to have over there!" observed Grizel. "What do you say, Gerry?"

"They are little horrors if they are like that," said Gerry firmly. "Sure you aren't exaggerating, any of you?"

"They are the rottenest lot I've ever known," declared Marie, who had picked up this expression from Margia, and thought this a good opportunity for airing it.

Mary turned to her, horror in her face. "Marie von Eschenau! Have you forgotten that you happen to be a sub?"

N-no-o-o," said Marie, rather crestfallen. "But it is true Mary."

"I daresay. You're not to use such language if it's true fifty times over."

"Well, what are we to do about this?" demanded Joey, as a means of changing the subject. "We can't go over and tackle them with it, as we're supposed to be more or less in quarantine, and though they did give us the wretched thing, still some of us might carry it to them when they wouldn't get it any other way. So what shall we do?"

That was settled for them by a summons from Mrs. Russell, who sent word that she wished to speak to them. They raced down, while Gerry and Grizel seated themselves and waited resignedly for what news might be forthcoming later on. They had plenty to discuss, for Gerry wanted to know all about the little Princess, and Grizel told the story of her coming to the school, and of the adventures she had had with Jo; and how Jo had rescued the little Princess, with the aid of Rufus the great St. Bernard dog, when she was lost.

"Just like Jo," said Grizel. "She's one of the best friends I have, and she's as straight as a die. I don't believe she could do a mean thing if she died for it! And whatever you trust to Jo, you know that it's done as well as she can do it."

Meanwhile the prefects had entered the *Speisesaal*, where Madge was waiting to speak to them. Jo, glancing at her sister's charming face, noted at once that she looked flushed and angry. Her eyes were very dark, and there was something in the set of her pretty lips that boded trouble for someone. She motioned them to come in and shut the door after them. They did so, glancing at each other in surprised question, for everyone had a clear conscience, and even Joey could think of nothing she had done that could call that look to her sister's face, though she racked her brains hurriedly on the subject.

"Sit down, girls," said the Head coldly.

They found seats, and all looked up at her as she stood in her short blue skirt and white jumper-blouse, looking very little older than Mary herself.

"I have had a letter from his Majesty, the King of Belsornia," she began, still in those icy tones. "He tells me that he has had an anonymous letter from here, saying that you are all talking of Elisaveta most disrespectfully. I wish to know, first of all, if any of you know anything about the letter?"

Jo stood up, fumbling at her pocket. "Yes; at least, I've had a letter from Elisaveta, and she tells me that someone has written from the Tiernsee, saying the same thing more or less to her."

"May I see your letter?" asked Madge. Jo handed it to her, and she glanced rapidly through its contents. Madge nodded. "Yes; I see. And you cannot help me at all, girls, in this matter?

They all shook their heads: but Mary, with a very red face, got up and said, "Madame, do you think — I — mean — we're not the only people here, are we?"

"What are you talking about?" demanded Madge.

"She means that there's more schools than one on the Tiernsee now," said Jo, coming to Mary's rescue.

Madge's face lightened. "You mean that you think that possibly some of the girls from St. Scholastika's did it as a joke?" she asked.

"I — I suppose so," said Joey.

"I see. I should be sorry to think that any of the Chalet girls could be so lost to all the dictates of good breeding as to write an anonymous letter. Apart from that, it would be most disloyal, since such statements might have a bad effect on the school.''

''There isn't a girl in the school, Madame, not the youngest of the juniors, who would do such a thing,'' said Mary earnestly.

The Head's charming smile flashed out. ''You are right there, I think, Mary. But if any of the girls from St. Scholastika's did such a silly thing, we must, I think forgive them. They could not realize what a dreadful thing they were doing in trying to harm another school in this way. You girls don't always think what trouble you may bring on yourselves and other people when you start feuds.''

''But, Madame, it takes two to make a quarrel,'' protested Simone.

''That is true, Simone. But at present, you must yield up your part in it. Really, girls, it is simply absurd the way you have all been behaving lately. There has been more back-biting and maliciousness in your conversation in this one term than in all the others of the Chalet School put together. It is a very wrong attitude. Also the younger ones all look up to you, and take their cue from you. If this goes on, you are going to harm them morally. I don't often preach, as you know, but I think that, on this occasion, I am justified.'' She glanced at the scarlet faces round her, and knew that her little 'preachment' had gone home.

''I am sorry, Madame,'' said Mary, lifting her eyes bravely. ''We didn't think.''

''No, Mary; that is so often the trouble. Now, with regard to this anonymous letter business, I must ask each girl if she knows anything about it. I know that I can trust you all to tell me the truth, and if I hear that no one has a hand in the matter I shall then know whom to blame. I must, of course, write to the King and tell him; but I shall ask that it goes no further, and I shall hope to find that next term you girls will have buried the hatchet.''

She dismissed them, but Joey paused after the others had gone. "Madge," she said, "*we* may say that we'll stop ragging — but what about *them*?"

"I think you will find that if you are not actively against them, they will cease to be actively against you. I don't expect miracles of friendliness in a few weeks, of course. That would be impossible. But I do hope that among you you will manage to put an end to a spirit such as the one that engendered this letter."

Jo nodded. Then she slipped an arm round her sister. "What a little *saint* you are, Madge," she breathed. Then, shy after such an unusual — for her — demonstration, she raced away.

CHAPTER TWENTY

The End of the Feud

"Vera Smithers, you are to go to Miss Browne *at once*!"

Vera looked up in surprise as Gipsy Carson came to the door of the senior common-room and flung this information at her.

"Did she say why, Gipsy?"

"More or less," said Gipsy coldly.

Something in her tone, but more in her attitude, sent a rush of colour to Vera's face, and then she went white, and something not unlike fear came into her eyes.

"What have you been up to, Vera?" asked Doris Potts laughingly.

"You'll know soon enough," said Gipsy sombrely. "You'd better go and get it over, Vera."

Vera turned and went to the door. Arrived there, she stopped suddenly, and came back. "Gipsy! Come with me!"

Gipsy cast her a look of scorn. "Turning coward?" she asked; and the girls wondered if those very icy tones *could* belong to merry Gipsy Carson.

At her words Vera flushed again. She let fall the hands she had outstretched in appeal and made her way out of the room, stumbling a little as she went. The rest sat in silence, for they had no idea what could have happened to make Gipsy speak like that, or Vera look as though something dreadful had happened. None of them liked to ask Gipsy, who had gone to the window and was standing there with her back to them. It was a particularly forbidding back, somehow, and Gipsy's whole attitude said quite plainly that she meant to answer no questions. With a curious feeling that something — it was tragedy, had they only known it — was in the air, they turned back to their pursuits, and Gipsy, after gazing unseeingly at the snow on the ground and the ice-black lake beyond, quietly left the room.

She went upstairs, and to her dormitory, where she wrapped herself in a duvet, and sat down on her bed to try and recover from the shock she had just received. She was very still, and though her eyes were bright with unshed tears she kept them back.

That afternoon, when she and Elaine and Elspeth had been lounging about in their form-room, Miss Browne herself had come in to get a copy of an arithmetic she had lent to their form the previous night. Elaine and Gipsy had not had it, and Elspeth had passed it on to someone else during the first twenty minutes of prep. There was nothing for it but to search the desks, and Miss Browne, not willing to take up the free time of the girls, had refused their help and hunted herself. Seeing that she really preferred to do it alone, they had turned back to their own concerns and had paid no further attention to her. She had gone along the front row of desks without finding the book she was seeking, and had passed from Maureen's empty desk to the one occupied by Vera Smithers. It was so untidy that it was impossible to see what was in it and what was not. With a mental resolve to send for Vera and give her a lecture, Miss Browne began to take the things out and pile them neatly on one side. The three girls were not noticing her, and no one troubled about her occupation. Miss Browne went on quietly and methodically till she had found her book, at the very bottom of the desk, under a welter of exercise-paper, atlas, sketch-books, and a light novel which had no business there − or in the building at all, as the Head-mistress knew after the first glance at its title. With the idea of confiscating it she picked it up, but held it so carelessly that she dropped it, and a number of slips of paper were shed on the floor. The girls turned at the sound of the falling book, but their movement to pick it up was checked by the unusual

168

look on their Head's face, and the almost fierce way in which she waved them back. "Stay where you are, girls!"

Half-startled, half-frightened, they did as she bade them. She picked up the papers, rummaged in the desk, and produced two or three more; then, with the two books and the slips in her hand, she went to the mistress's desk in the corner, and stood by it, looking over her find. "Come here," she said at length.

They came, wondering at her tone. She pointed to the papers, and on them they saw various attempts at script-writing, and sentences that made them open their eyes.

"I see you know to what these bits of paper refer," said the Head-mistress, an unusual rasp in her voice. "May I ask which of you had to do with those disgraceful anonymous letters to the King of Belsornia and the Crown Princess?"

They all stared at her in amazement. Gipsy had a private doubt as to Miss Browne's sanity, and Elspeth wondered if she were ill. Only Elaine knew anything about it, and she went red and gave a little gasp.

Miss Browne was down on her in a flash. "Yes, Elaine! What do you know about these? Was it you who were responsible for such a shameless thing?"

But Elaine met the angry eyes fronting hers quite fearlessly. "I didn't do it, Miss Browne, if that is what you mean."

"But you had something to do with it?" asked Miss Browne.

"I — I am afraid the first idea was mine," stammered Elaine.

Miss Browne looked at her, utter contempt in her face. "You, my head-girl, could suggest such a contemptible thing as writing an anonymous letter to anyone? And to the King of Belsornia of all people! May I ask what you hoped to gain by it?"

Elaine had nothing to say. Her head sank lower and lower and her cheeks were scarlet.

"But what is it all about please, Miss Browne?" asked Gipsy, bewildered.

"Mrs Russell, who is titular Head of the Chalet School, rang me up today to say that the King of Belsornia, whose little daughter, the Crown Princess Elisaveta, was, for two terms, a pupil at the Chalet School, had received a letter from the Tiernsee, accusing the girls of the Chalet School of speaking of her Highness most disrespectfully. The letter was anonymous, and he, thinking it to be meant as a poor joke on the part of some of her former school-fellows, sent it back to Mrs Russell, reminding her that such a thing, had it fallen into other hands than his own, might have brought great discredit on the school. Mrs Russell made instant inquiries among her girls, but they have all assured her that they knew nothing about it. She rang me up to tell me of it, and to ask if I thought any of ours could have played such a silly practical joke. I was so sure of the sense of honour prevailing here that I assured her that none of our girls would have lowered themselves or their school by behaving in such a way, and she accepted my word. It appears that I spoke too soon. But I shall punish this most severely. We have not been so friendly with the Chalet School as we ought, and I can see that I am to blame myself for part of the friction between you. But I never expected, or even dreamt, that such friction could bring any of you as low as this.

''That one of my girls — and a senior girl, too — could stoop to such petty maliciousness in order to damage the reputation of a school against which she had a grudge, is something I find hard to believe, even now. That you, Elaine, my head-girl, could even have made such a suggestion, shows to what an extent you have fallen.

''I must see Vera Smithers at once, and find out how much she knows about this. Gipsy, will you please find her, and tell her to come to me in my study now. Elaine, you had better come with me, I think. Elspeth, please put those things back into the desk tidily.''

She left the room, followed by a white-faced Elaine, and Gipsy had gone to give her message to Vera, and then slipped off, as has been seen, after a decent time had elapsed for the girl to reach the Head's study.

Gipsy Carson had had less to do with that silly 'feud' than any other girl in the school, but the Head's words had gone deep with her. Sitting there on her bed, she told herself miserably that part of it must be her fault, for if she had withstood Elaine and Vera in their attitude to the Chaletians, it would have died down sooner, and then this would not have occurred. "It *is* my fault, as much as anyone else's," she told herself. "I knew it was all wrong to feel like that about them, but I just didn't bother — just drifted, as Mr Eastley said on Sunday in his sermon. It was the easiest thing to do, so I did it, just as I always *do* do the easiest thing."

Elspeth came to seek her presently, and to her Gipsy said much the same thing. "I've always been a drifter, Elspeth. And this is where it's landed me!"

Elspeth was comforting. "I don't think anything you could have done would have made much difference to Vera, Gipsy. You won't know this, but she tried to be friendly with Joey Bettany and Marie von Eschenau — extra friendly, I mean; and they would have nothing to do with her. She wanted to get Marie to ask her to stay at Vienna, because Marie's father is a nobleman, if he used his title, and because Joey knows such heaps of nice people. They were very crushing to her, and she vowed she would be revenged on them. It was not your fault that Vera is as she is."

"But I might have helped," groaned Gipsy. "But I just laughed, and let things slide. It is no use, Elspeth! I may not be directly to blame for this; but you heard what Mr Eastley said. We all have a certain amount of influence over our fellows, and it must be for good or evil. My influence over Vera was not for good — I'm certain of *that*! So it must have been for evil."

Elspeth said what she could; but just at present Gipsy was

facing things seriously for almost the first time in her life, and she was not ready for consolation.

Meanwhile, downstairs in the study, Miss Browne was facing something different. Elaine had been sorry and ashamed; but Vera, on her way to judgment, had made up her mind that it was not worth while to show any feelings of that kind, even if she had had it. She was sorry that she had been found out — and she knew, when Gipsy had delivered the message that she *was* found out — but of shame for her disgraceful act she felt none. She supposed there would be a fuss, but she had weathered storms before, and though they were uncomfortable they had been nothing worse. So she met Miss Browne's eyes with an impudent defiance that told the Head that nothing could be done here by gentleness or lenience. The best thing for Vera was the severest punishment she could inflict, so that the shock of it might awaken her to what she had been doing.

"You know why I have sent for you, Vera?" asked the Headmistress.

"I suppose so," said Vera nonchalantly.

Miss Browne spread the slips before her on the desk. "Was it you who wrote those anonymous letters to the King and Crown Princess of Belsornia?"

Vera glanced at them. "Not much use saying I didn't when you've found out that I did, is there?" she retorted flippantly.

Miss Browne rose to her feet. "Vera," she said sternly, "do you quite realize what this means? Are you aware of the fact that you have been cowardly — dishonourable — unladylike — though that last matters least. Your breach of good manners is the smallest thing in all this trouble. And what is this book doing in the school?" she went on, lifting it from her desk. "You know that you are all forbidden to read any of this author's works while you are at school. There is a reason for that, Vera. We want you girls to retain your purity of mind as long as possible. Do you think that you can soil your minds with the thoughts and deeds recorded in such a story and yet retain that purity? You are not little children now. Yet you, a senior, can break my rule in this deliberate manner.''

"I don't see why we shouldn't read what we like," mumbled Vera. In spite of herself, the Head's manner was beginning to take effect.

"Is that really true?" asked Miss Browne quietly.

The girl raised her eyes, which, despite her resolution, had fallen, and tossed back the soft fair hair from her face. "Oh well, I knew there would be a row," she said.

"Is that all you have to say for yourself?"

Vera glanced across at Elaine. "Well," she began spitefully. "I *might* say that I hadn't had the best of examples set me by the head-girl —"

"Silence!" said Miss Browne sternly. "Don't add to your fault by laying the blame of this on someone else's shoulders. Elaine has to answer to me for her shortcomings; but with all her errors, Vera, she has been above the meanness of accusing another girl of influencing her wrongly."

There was a little silence after that. Vera had shot her bolt and was beginning to feel very uncomfortable. She had been in trouble over and over again, but this seemed somehow worse than usual. Miss Browne had never been quite like this before.

Then the Head spoke again. "Go to your room, Elaine," she said. "I will come to you there."

Elaine went in utter silence, but her lips were trembling and her eyes were full of tears.

Left alone with the Head, Vera looked at her uneasily.

"Now, Vera," said Miss Browne briskly, "you must see for yourself how bad things are with you. You have expressed no sorrow for all that you have done — you lead me to believe that your one grief is that you have been found out. For the sake of the school's good name, for the sake of your companions, but most of all for your own sake, I can keep you here no longer."

173

Vera started. She had not expected this. The defiance and impudence slipped away, leaving her what she was in reality — a school-girl who had forgotten most of the laws that govern the life of every honourable school-girl, and who was beginning to find that she could not break these laws with impunity.

"I will not make it public expulsion," continued Miss Browne, "but I shall write to your parents, laying all the facts of the case before them, and telling them that I can no longer receive you in this school."

With a rush Vera flung herself on her knees before the Head. "Oh, Miss Browne not that — not that!" she gasped. "Oh, you *can't* send me away for just that letter and bringing a forbidden book into school — it wouldn't be fair! Oh, Miss Browne, forgive me — forgive me!"

"Get up, Vera," said Miss Browne. "You must never kneel to a human being. As for forgiving you," she went on, more gently, "I forgive you your sin against me, but I cannot have your influence in the school. I must think of the other girls and their welfare. The many cannot suffer for the one. Besides, Vera, it seems to me that this may be the turning-point in your life. I dare not be lenient with you. We have tried lenience before, and this is all that has come of it. Now, we must see what severity will do for you. It is not a pleasant thing for me to have to do. In all the years that I have kept a school I have never had to send away a girl before. Nor should I now, if I did not think that, by bringing home to you the depth to which you have descended, by punishing you in this way, I am doing you a service."

She stopped speaking, and looked at Vera. The girl's face had a sullen expression, and there was no repentance in her looks. Miss Browne waited to hear if she had anything more to say; but Vera knew now that there was no hope of persuading the Head to change her sentence, and she was determined to say nothing more. She remained in the school for two days

174

longer, during which time she was in solitary confinement. The girls were told that Vera Smithers had disgraced himself and her school, and was not coming back again. An escort was found to take her to England, and she departed without expressing any further sorrow for what she had done. Miss Browne was right. The only thing she regretted was being found out.

As for Elaine, after a long interview with the Head, at which she had cried till she could hardly see, she was forgiven and given another chance. Her punishment was to be solitary confinement for two days. At the end of that time she came out, a very different girl from the one who had urged on the feud against the Chalet School, and, for the rest of the year which was left to her at St Scholastika's, she did her best to put an end to all ill-feeling against the Chaletians. Perhaps she found her greatest help in the Guide Company that was formed at the beginning of the next term. Miss Browne, convinced at last that the girls needed Guides, withdrew her veto on them, and Miss Soames and Miss Elliott were given their way in that matter at last.

"So it was them after all," said Joey Bettany thoughtfully, when Madge told her briefly what had happened.

"No," said Madge unexpectedly. "It was you as well, Joey. If you girls had not taken up the feud as you did, and carried it out as far as you did, the chances are that none of this would have happened."

Marie, Simone, Mary, and Frieda, released at last from the sick-room, looked up at this.

"Then it was our faults too?" said Simone.

"I think so. But it is at an end now. Next term, when they have begun Guides, you can begin again, and this time it will be as comrades, and not rivals."

"I suppose we *were* rather kiddish," said Mary. "There really is room for the two schools here, and as they only take

175

English girls, and most of ours are from other countries, we ought not to get in one another's way."

"Quite true," said Mrs Russell.

The call came for Frieda to go and get ready to go home to Innsbruck. Bernhilda's wedding was to take place two days hence, and, after that, school would begin very soon. The girls had all been at the Sonnalpe for the holidays, for Marie was to be one of Bernhilda's bridesmaids, and it was too far for Simone to go home by herself.

When Frieda had gone with Gottfried, followed by many promises from the others to be sure to turn up for the wedding, and when Marie and Simone had run off to visit Marie's pretty sister-in-law, Gisela, the first head-girl of the Chalet School, while Mary went to fulfil a promise to the Robin to read *Peter Pan* to her, Jo turned to her sister. "On the whole, I think I'm jolly glad we're going to be friends," she said seriously. "It's such a bore to have to remember all the time that you aren't pals with someone! I like Gipsy and Elspeth already, and I expect the others are jolly nice too, when you get to know them."

Madge burst out laughing as she got up to go to David, who was yelling lustily for her. "Oh, Joey Bettany!" she retorted. "Will you ever grow up?"

THE END